we

are

GOLD

GOLD

we

are

GOLD

ALICE CHAMBERS

NEW
ISLAND

For Michele,
something for
your
Swoon
Suitcase! Hope
you enjoy it.
x Alice

We Are Gold
First published 2007
by New Island
2 Brookside
Dundrum Road
Dublin 14

www.newisland.ie

ISBN   978-1-905494-58-3

British Library Cataloguing in Publication Data.
A CIP catalogue record for this book is available from the British Library.

Printed in the UK by Athenaeum Press Ltd., Gateshead, Tyne & Wear
Cover design by Inka Hagen

10 9 8 7 6 5 4 3 2 1

For Donal and Maeve

A Child's Things

by Rose Gold

Here lies the bucket
Here, the spade
Here is the castle
With gothic façade

There are the melon pips
Left out to dry
Here is the necklace
You'll make by and by

These are the pebbles
You painted and glued
Here is your dolls house
And miniature zoo

Here are your sequins
Your glitter
Your pens
Your stickers
Your witches
Your secrets
Your shells

Your fancy notepaper
Your Popsicle maker
Your bubbles
Your hairbrush
Your puppet theatre

Those ladybird buttons
That blue dressing gown
These paper umbrellas
That pink eiderdown

Your skipping rope
Coiled
Like that stuffed orange snake
Those hundreds and thousands
Your ninth birthday cake

Your will o' the wisp
Your didgeridoo
Your straw hat
Your eyes wide
Your pigtails askew

These things remain
But the child is gone.

Hannah Gold

Hannah Gold, 23 years old, died in a car crash on a cold February morning. Daughter of Rose and Henry Gold. Elder sister of Omega and Dawn. Mother of Jack.

She was buried following a small ceremony at the Golds' local church.

In the days after the funeral, Jack kept asking where she was. And Rose told him she was on holidays in heaven, with the angels. But then Jack started to cry and ask why she had preferred to go there rather than stay with him. And there was no answering that question.

Time to Go

Rose was sitting at the kitchen table, putting the finishing touches to her daily poem. Henry was leaning against the kitchen sink at the window that overlooked the back garden. He stood contemplating his Paris daisies and a robin that had just then alighted on the gooseberry bushes; their prickly shadow danced on the terracotta pots of red and pink geraniums scattered below. The robin cocked an inquisitive eye in Henry's direction. Henry blinked. Rose stole a look at her husband's face in profile; his expression was inscrutable in the early morning light, the sun's rays bouncing off his spectacles.

Jack appeared in the doorway, tousled and sleepy. He wandered silently over to the sink like he was sleep-walking and tugged at Henry's trousers. Henry set down his mug and lifted Jack up. 'Look,' he said.

Jack stirred with sudden excitement. 'It's the wobbin!' he shouted. 'The wobbin's back!'

Henry and Rose exchanged a brief smile, interrupted by Dawn.

'I'm late!' she announced breathlessly to no one in particular, flouncing theatrically into the room.

'For a very important date?' enquired Rose, amused as always by her youngest daughter's innate sense of quotidian drama.

'Har, har,' said Dawn, pulling a face and rolling her hazel eyes skywards.

'No time to say hello, goodbye,' rejoined Henry, gently putting Jack down, who greeted this relegation with mild protest.

Dawn, meanwhile, had poured herself a cup of coffee and was reaching for the cornflakes in the cupboard overhead. 'Where's Hannah?' she asked through crunches.

'Down any minute now,' Rose said automatically.

'I wish she'd bloody hurry up. I'm going to be late.' Henry arched an eyebrow at Rose, meaning: since when has Dawn been worried about being late for school?

Dawn caught him and glared balefully at them both. Unaccountably, Jack giggled. Dawn's features relaxed into a sheepish grin. She reached over and ruffled Jack's hair. 'What about you, monster? Are you ready for your big trip to the zoo? Better be careful or they'll leave you in the cage with all the other monkeys!' Jack giggled good-humouredly.

The most balanced member of the family, thought Rose.

Hannah still hadn't appeared five minutes later. Dawn glanced at her watch again and chewed the nail of her right index finger savagely.

'Don't bite your nails, dear,' said Rose from the kitchen table, although Dawn could have sworn she hadn't once looked up from her notebook. *Could her mother hear her biting her nails from across the room?* Dawn wondered.

Henry cleared his throat and ventured out of the kitchen into the hallway. Dawn could see his reflection in the mirror looking upwards through the wind chime, in the general direction of Hannah's attic enclave. 'Hannah?' he said, almost to himself. Not even the robin, had he been within twenty yards, would have heard him.

Dawn yelped in irritation and bounced off her stool at the island counter. 'Hannah!' she yelled with blood-curdling menace.

'Not so loud, dear,' pleaded Rose, her pen poised in mid-air, her mind a sudden blank. *The word, what was that word?* She'd had it. Now it was gone.

'Coming!' rebounded an equally loud yell, followed by several deafening bangs and the sound of steps being taken two at a time.

Now it was Hannah who appeared in the doorway, brushing past Henry, still standing vaguely at the banisters. She glowered first at Dawn and then in the general direction of the world and everything it contained.

'Keep your hair on,' she snarled menacingly in her sister's direction.

Dawn, unruffled, said, 'Move it.'

Ignoring her, Hannah swooped on Jack and enveloped him in a bear hug. 'Ready?' she asked, hunkering down.

'Yep,' he answered, adding, 'the wobbin's back!'

'Wow!' said Hannah with the right degree of enthusiasm. 'See?' she said teasingly. 'He always comes back.'

Jack nodded solemnly and a kind of pact between them was sealed tighter. He had been distraught when the bird disappeared last summer, despite his grandfather's best efforts to reassure him. Only Hannah had been able to find the right words.

'You believe in Santa, right?' she'd asked him.

Jack assented.

'And me?' she'd said, suddenly scared. Jack nodded vigorously. 'So if I tell you he'll he back, he'll be back. It's as simple as that.' Jack had nodded once more and buried his head in her chest.

Later on, Rose had gently suggested to Hannah that Jack might be somehow identifying the absence of any father figure in his life with the absent robin. Hannah had struggled with this for a moment before conceding that she may have had a point.

'But,' said Rose, keenly aware of a thousand and one things, 'you handled it so well. I was proud of you.'

Hannah gave her a tearful grin. 'Thanks, Mum,' she said. 'You didn't handle us so badly yourself.'

'Ready?' Dawn snarled.

Hannah sighed and shrugged. 'Sure,' she said, 'let's go.'

'Goodbye, then,' Rose said, not looking up from her notebook. 'See you later.'

Hannah grabbed her car keys from the counter and bent over to kiss Rose's cheek on the way out.

'Let me read it later?' she asked. It was a kind of routine private joke between the two. Rose never let anyone read her poems. It was the only thing she really felt was her own. It wasn't egotism, exactly; more like an act of self-preservation. But uncharacteristically, Rose looked up and met Hannah's gaze.

'You know what?' she said to her eldest daughter. 'I think I might just let you read them all.'

'Wow!' said Hannah, genuinely surprised. She had been asking the same question for years and the answer had always been no. 'What did I do to deserve that?' she laughed, catching Henry's eye, who smiled back.

'Well, maybe it's time,' said Rose airily, smiling broadly and feeling unaccountably light hearted.

'So why can't I read it now?' Hannah suddenly demanded. 'Before you change your mind?'

'For God's sake, Hannah!' screeched Dawn. 'We are *sooooo* late.'

Hannah glanced at the wall clock. 'All right, all right,' she conceded, turning once more towards Rose. 'Bye, Dad,' she said, passing Henry at the doorway.

'Bye, love,' he answered. 'Bye, Jack, bye, Dawn, have a good day.'

When they were gone, Henry couldn't resist asking Rose. 'What made you say that?'

'I don't know,' she answered truthfully. 'I guess it just felt like it was time.'

Goodbye, Omega

The last time Omega saw Hannah, they met at the Screen cinema on D'Olier Street. The familiar squat bronze usher shone his dull torch unperturbed, confident that against all odds it would shed light on the moviegoers.

Hannah arrived breathless and apologetic.

'Jack was sick,' she explained hurriedly as her brother stuffed the ticket into her hand. 'I couldn't leave him.'

'No worries', said Omega, holding the door open for her. 'It's good to see you, sis.' Hannah smiled at him and stepped inside.

When they came out, it was already dark. The crowd drifted towards the door, reluctant to leave the dreamy other world of the cinema.

'What did you think?' asked Omega.

'I thought it was stilted,' replied Hannah. 'The characters were too wooden, the dialogue was too hesitant, too...' she frowned, searching for the right word. 'Cowardly.'

Omega nodded, pretending to understand.

They strolled down the street in companionable silence.

'Hannah,' Omega interjected suddenly. 'I'm thinking of asking Cristelle to marry me.'

'My God!' Hannah teased. 'Are you sure? I mean, don't you think it's a bit sudden? You've only been together for what ... seven years? How could you possibly make such a hasty decision?'

'Very funny,' said Omega, giving her a playful shove. She shoved back. He shoved her again. She shoved harder. They both laughed and held their palms up, signalling a truce.

Omega suddenly looked serious. 'We'd love you to sing for us at the – you know - ceremony.'

'Try and stop me,' Hannah replied.

They hugged.

'I'd better get going,' Hannah said finally. 'Relieve the grandparents from babysitting duty.'

She turned to leave but just before she did, she looked back and wagged her index finger at him in a threatening manner. 'This is my best buddy we're talking about here, treat her right or you'll have me to answer to.'

As it turned out, that was the last thing she ever said to him.

Best Friends Forever

When the Golds were growing up, it was not unusual for neighbours to talk about Omega and his three sisters. This popular, but erroneous, perception was not entirely without justification. In the wonderful lottery that is childhood, Cristelle and Hannah wound up extracting each other's numbers from the chance machine and were placed side by side on day one in primary school. Years afterwards Rose said she'd never forget how, when she had tearfully gone to hug her first daughter goodbye, the little blonde girl in the next seat had suddenly reached out and patted her on the arm.

'Don't worry,' the girl had said in what had struck Rose as a very serious, grown-up voice.

Rose tore herself away from Hannah, while Hannah steadfastly ignored her in what would be the first of many characteristic shows of fierce independence. Cristelle, meanwhile, waved and smiled at Rose all the way out the door. Rose – touched by this little girl's big heart – waved back.

During the break Cristelle offered Hannah some of her iced gems; the coloured blobs of icing stood like tiny Russian minarets on their biscuit foundations. Hannah responded by slipping five hula-hoops on her fingers and licking them until they disintegrated and broke. She counted out five more for Cristelle.

By the end of the day, they were friends for life.

Red Lorry, Yellow Lorry

Hannah was driving.

Dawn was in the passenger seat and Jack was strapped into the back directly behind her.

As they approached the crossroads, the light changed from amber to green. Dawn glanced at Hannah and sang along with the radio, '*There ain't no stopping us no-ow-oooo-ow-ow.*'

Hannah grinned and, briefly taking her left hand off the steering wheel, punched her sister playfully on the shoulder. None of them saw the lorry hurtling through the red light to their left. All they felt was the impact, the weird sensation of the car sailing over their heads and their bodies tumbling through time and space.

Someone, either Dawn or Hannah, cried out. But Dawn could never remember which one of them it was.

The doctors said Hannah died instantly.

Damage

Dawn emerged with two fractured ribs and a broken nose. Jack, miraculously, emerged unscathed. At least physically. Afterwards, it was a year before he put a full sentence together.

Some time later the ambulance men confessed to Rose that they'd had a hard time of it when they got to the scene of the crash. They'd found Dawn thrashing around violently in her seat, her legs banging frantically on the roof of the car. She kept screaming at them that she was fine and that they needed to get Hannah out: '*Now!*'

But Hannah had already been cut loose.

There was a good ten minutes, they said, where Dawn kept shouting and pointing frantically to the empty space beside her. The only explanation in medical terms was that her eyes had somehow stopped working; the last image of Hannah was imprinted on her retina and time hadn't yet spooled forward.

Someone else had managed to extricate Jack. He was sitting on the side of the road like a little ghost, an emergency blanket draped over his shoulders. His body shook uncontrollably. When they tried to take him to the ambulance, he refused to move. It took two grown men to finally prise him away from the pavement. Even then, he put up a ferocious resistance. Dawn could hear him screaming the entire way there. It was only when they shut the ambulance doors that her body went limp – from sheer exhaustion – and they were able to ease her out.

It was the thought of Jack alone in the ambulance that finally got through to her. Hannah wouldn't have wanted him to be alone with strangers.

The Unravelling

'Mr Gold?'

He saw a shadowy figure through the oblong stained glass panels in the front door.

'Mr Gold?'

Henry didn't say anything.

There was a long silence.

The person on the other side of the door coughed and, reaching up, appeared to remove a hat of some sort from his head.

'Mr Gold. Can you let me in?'

Henry automatically went to open the latch and then inexplicably let his hand fall limp to his side.

'Mr Gold. Can you hear me?'

Henry heard himself say yes, a disembodied yes that came from some remote location within his head.

'This is Officer Sheehy, Mr Gold. I'm afraid there's been an accident. I...your...Mr Gold, can I come in?'

Henry was already halfway back down the hall, putting on his coat, when Rose emerged from the kitchen.

'Accident,' Henry managed to mouth but not quite

say. 'Police,' he mimed helplessly, pointing wildly off target in the direction of the wall.

Rose half-walked, half-fell towards him. Henry caught her just in time.

'Please,' she managed to whisper. 'No.' She was clutching the edge of his coat.

'Rose,' Henry said, placing his hands firmly on both her shoulders and looking her straight in the eyes. 'We have to go now. They need us.'

Rose nodded dumbly.

Henry half-escorted, half-manhandled her to the car.

The Phone Call

Omega was in work. He saw Ciara the receptionist pick up the phone, listen and blanch visibly. She stared in his direction. He felt vaguely flattered, then alarmed. He waved at her and pulled a comic face, but her facial muscles had frozen. The hair on the nape of his neck began to tingle. When the phone on his desk rang, he jumped like he'd been hit by lightning.

'Omega?' said a familiar voice. It was Rose. Relief flooded through him. 'Where's Cristelle?'

Omega's hair started prickling again. His collar felt uncomfortably tight. He fiddled with his biro. Rose broke in again, her voice more urgent this time.

'Where's Cristelle, Omega?'

'She's in the flat, I think,' he said, feeling puzzled. 'Last time I saw her,' he added. 'What's up, Mum? You sound kind of spooked.'

There was silence on the other end of the phone.

'Mum?' Omega repeated, jigging his right knee under the desk. In the background, he thought he heard his father say something. *But his father was at work.* He pressed the receiver to his right ear. *Was that traffic in the background?*

'Mum, are you in a car?' Omega asked. 'Is that Dad with you?'

'We're on our way to St Vincent's Hospital,' she said in a weirdly efficient tone, like she was reading the weather report. 'Come now and contact Cristelle. Tell her to come too. 'It's—' Omega felt a sudden acute pain of unknown origin in his chest '—a car accident.'

At that moment, Mr Fitzsimmons emerged from his office and shouted, 'Omega, get in here!' Omega half-waved at him, half-swatted him away. Mr Fitzsimmons took that to mean yes. He wouldn't have known what no looked like if it walked up and shook hands with him. 'Presto!' he snapped irritably. 'Today, not next week,' and disappeared into his office. Omega got up and walked over to Ciara. He pointed mutely at Mr Fitzsimmons's office and she nodded briefly to show she'd understood; her right index finger was already dialling his extension as Omega shrugged on his coat and yanked the door shut behind him.

What to Do

Some time after Hannah's death, Rose asked Henry what people meant when they said: 'I suppose you just have to get on with things.'

'What kinds of things, Henry,' she said, 'are they supposing I'm meant to be getting on with?'

'People are just trying to be kind,' he told her.

'I know,' she persisted, 'but what are these "things" I should be doing?'

'Oh, Rose,' said Henry wearily. 'These "things" you keep talking about are life without Hannah. They're the sum total of our world without her in it. It's an equation, Rose: people mean get on with everything minus her. They also mean you have no choice in the matter. We do have two other children, you know, and a grandson.'

'I haven't forgotten that,' she snapped at him. 'But I wish someone would bloody tell me what these things they keep going on about are exactly.'

'I just tried, Rose,' said Henry patiently. 'But you don't want to listen.'

Four Years Later

Omega came home and sensed he was not alone. He went into the kitchen and poured himself a glass of milk. He was thinking about checking his answering machine and taking a shower when the presence of a little tattered note stuck to the fridge door manifested itself from across the room.

He observed it between sips, from a distance.

For some reason its diminutive presence on the fridge's clean white surface inspired a certain tenderness in him. From where he was standing, it seemed to be apologising for this sudden invasion into his mental and physical space. And this impression, the moment it had been formed, was immediately replaced by another, more forcible one. What initially struck Omega as a sorry, grubby sight was somehow transformed into the very opposite. The note, as it now appeared to him, had not only taken up a prominent central position on his fridge door, but it had done so in the style of Custer's Last Stand. Everything about its existence suggested tenacity and the will to prevail. By the time Omega realised he would rather not have seen it at all, it was too late. His first impression, he thought gloomily, was right: he had company.

A minute passed. Omega and the note stared at each other, separated by the perfectly symmetrical black and white floor tiles.

The note won.

Cradling the now empty glass in his left hand, Omega reluctantly gave in to its superior will. He walked crossword-like across the kitchen to the fridge, five across, ten down (*piano, pianissimo*).

'Oh hello there, note,' he ventured.

'GO TO HELL,' the note spat back at him. 'I'm leaving you,' it added.

Omega saw the words, but hadn't processed them yet.

A few seconds passed.

Gone, he finally thought.

'Not happy at all. Taking my stuff and going away,' he translated for the sake of clarity.

The note hung there, sucked into the fridge's body by the cow-shaped made-in-Hong-Kong magnet which not only performed this gravity-defying service but also mooed when pressure was applied to its black and white stomach. And this is what the cow now did as Omega attempted to prise the note out from under its udders. It mooed.

He placed the offensive scrap of paper on the kitchen table, belly up. It was almost as though by putting it there and observing it anew from this altered perspective, the contents might appear different, might reveal themselves to him in a less definitive-sounding way. But no. MOO. The note looked up at him, unblinking. And just to be sure, he read it again, like a child might, pronouncing each syllable with exaggerated care. GO – TO – HELL. I – AM – LEAV – ING – YOU.

Never the brightest of the pack, Omega was nonetheless not a complete idiot and this second, more considered reading, even from this lofty height, was enough to convince him that his life had taken a turn for the worse.

He scooped up his cappuccino-coloured coat, his wallet, his house keys, and pausing only for the time it took him to locate his umbrella and transfer it to his left hand, fled from the fridge's white glare. Out of the kitchen. Into the pub.

Omega's Mother

Rose settled down to write her daily poem. It was a ritual that had become as important to her as any other in her days: one of the 'things' she had learned to get on with. A poem, she never tired of telling Omega, was once described as 'a momentary stay against confusion'. She wasn't sure who said this – Frost? Auden, perhaps? But then, she added, it didn't matter who said it, she had made the motto her own. Sometimes she even thought that *she* may have said it first.

Anyhow, this is what floated to mind.

Monday – The Flowerman

The Flowerman
Has one tooth in his head
It sprouts out of his gums
Like the first snowdrop
In spring
And he tells me it must be destiny
That we meet at this shop corner
Surrounded by the Latin-sounding names
Of his fresh-cut flowers.

She was pleased with her efforts. She puzzled a little over 'Latin-sounding names' (either they were Latin names or they weren't), but decided not to be pedantic about it. At least not today.

The Golds: A Brief History

Omega Gold was the second-last child. The last one was unplanned.

'What's unplanned?' asked Jack.

'Not part of the big plan,' Mr Gold always replied. He said it so often, it was as if Dawn had a different last name to everyone else: Dawn Not-Part-of-the-Big-Plan Gold.

'What Big Plan?' asked Jack.

'ShutupJack.' (Omega and Dawn in unison.)

Jack shut up.

Next time, he thought, he would frame the question differently.

Not Part of the Big Plan

Dawn (Not Part of the Big Plan) Gold was busy writing a letter. A letter she knew she would never send, but nonetheless felt she needed to write. And so she began. The words made the slow journey from liquid thought to concrete reality.

Dublin, late September 2006

Dear José-Maria,

How are you? Perhaps I'm embarking on a most perilous act in writing to you. I vividly remember you telling me once about a postcard you received from one of your 'exes' which occasioned nothing more than intense irritation on your part. As far as I recall she filled up most of the white rectangle with reasons why her world was infinitely better without you in it. (And you said her writing was *tiny*.) Do you remember?

Well, that is not my intention.

It's late and I don't know if I'll send this – great letter writing cliché – but I rather think I will, because if nothing else, I cannot get you out of my head and putting my thoughts down on paper gives me the illusion of freedom from my enslavement to you, temporary shelter from the storm in my heart.

I will tell you honestly that when I finally arrived home I felt numb. Which is to say, I was incapable of feeling anything any more. For a long time. Now that I've regained some of my sense of humour, I merely refer to our brief sojourn together as 'my biggest mistake ever'. (Ha ha.)

But mostly I feel sad. Really sad. Part of me wants to get angry, part of me to run after you. But you didn't turn back (it's a metaphor, José) and I am still struggling to understand what went so wrong, turned so sour (*crossed out turned so sour – made her feel like a lemon*).

I have no doubt that time will speed me away to different feelings, new encounters, but I'm terribly scared of getting close to someone again and risking obtuse silence and final definitive rejection.

That would be tough.

So maybe you could give me some road signs for the future? (How about when you suggested I buy a one-way ticket at Christmas?) 'It's a good prize,' you said. I think you meant price. Do you remember? Or have you buried this memory alongside the other debris that is now our relationship? (*Mental note to self: when your fiancé suggests you buy a one-way ticket and they do not reside in the city of destination, it ought to be read like a sign. A gigantic, brightly lit neon sign creaking in the wind outside a dusty old motel in deepest night.*)

But it's the whys of these things that torment me. Why this irrevocable retreat? Why this deafening silence? Why? Why? Why?

(*SHUT UP DAWN!*)

I hope you are well. Not. I have no idea what course your life has taken. What course has your life taken? By the way, I don't accept your lame theory on long-distance relationships! I still believe that what we had was unique. In fact, I actively dislike the attempt you made in your last communication to trivialise and homogenise it, stirring it into the bland porridge of all failed long-distance relationships for all time. (*Not convinced by bland porridge.*)

So post-Spain, apart from weeping at the most inconvenient times and places, I have by degrees managed to pull the threads of my existence together. I think I'm safe in saying that I am now tolerably well. I have also had a vision regarding my future. I plan to meet someone in due course, get engaged, get married, have some kids and buy a semi-detached red-brick Victorian house in some leafy suburb in Dublin. Which rules you out in almost all respects. We are no longer together (that covers points 2 and 3), you, quote, 'hate kidz', and for as long as I've known you you haven't had two pesos to rub together. (*I know, I know, you have the euro, it's called artistic licence.*)

I tell you about my vision because it feels bound up in the time we spent together and of course I'd be lying if I didn't say that I also burn from an intense desire to let you know that I'm doing fine – without you – all things considered.

I think that's all.

Regards to the cat.

If you're wondering why my English has gone all funny, it's because of a book I've just been reading.

I have no idea of what is the best way to sign off.

Maybe I'll just say goodbye.

Goodbye then.

xxxxx Aurora

The Gloaming

A tall willowy girl made her way along Boulevard
Saint-Germain. Her bright red suede Birkenstocks
had turned crimson. Her beige A-line three-quarter
length jacket looked and felt like a wet newspaper
clinging to her skin. Her mascara turned out not to be
waterproof. She walked and cried in the rain. She
thought about all the wasted water being produced by
her and the sky, and how contemporary political and
economic analysts said that water was now one of the
earth's most precious resources; how the wars of the
future would be fought for the control of its supplies;
how it was destined to become incredibly precious –
more precious even than oil or land or *gold*...

Christ.

She combed a distracted hand through her damp
hair. Her thoughts kept creeping up on her the same
way the puddles crept up to her feet, catching her
unawares. She pictured a hamster in its cage, running
on its tiny treadmill, treading the same mental
landscape over and over again. She stared at the
image in her mind, horrified. The hamster was
wearing crimson Birkenstocks and had an Alice band
in its hair.

She walked swiftly past the cars, wheezing along in the Friday night traffic. And thought, *Omega Gold: total bastard.* And felt a little better.

Omega's Fantasies

When Omega was small, he was perfectly convinced that he would be the first Irishman on the moon. This dream of his made him an unwitting constant source of amusement to the grown-ups. When asked to perform a party trick, he would simply look very disdainfully at his audience and say, 'One small step for man, one giant leap for mankind.' Sometimes he would continue, 'Houston! Houston! We've got a problem,' making loud interference noises that came somewhere from the back of his throat. 'Houston! This is Texas, come in, Houston, can you hear me?' As an adolescent, he discovered David Bowie and Pink Floyd and treated his family to a non-stop repeat play of 'Spaceman' and 'Comfortably Numb'. He was fond of responding to perfectly normal questions with cryptic quotes: 'There is no pain, you are receding, like distant ship smoke on the horizon' or 'You are only coming through in waves, your lips move but I cannot hear what you're saying.' He would write these quotes in indelible ink on his schoolbag. He watched *Star Trek* and took out a subscription to a monthly science magazine. One year when he got back from school he discovered that his bedroom walls were literally covered in star stickers and that his lamp had been transformed into a rocket. There was even a giant moon painted above his bed. Cristelle had asked Mrs Gold if she'd help her do it as a surprise for his birthday. It was a defining moment in their relationship. After he realised it was improbable that he would be the first Irishman on the moon, he turned to the study of astrophysics. His new dream was to chart hitherto unknown star systems and galaxies. He found an article entitled 'Composition of the Cosmos' and was so struck by it that he learned it off by heart and would often be heard quoting it to friends who needed some perspective in their lives. He'd take out a pen and paper and draw a diagram, and once he was sure that he'd got their attention, take a deep breath and intone: 'This diagram shows the ingredients that make up the universe. Astronomers now realise that the universe's main ingredient is *dark energy*, a mysterious form of energy that exists between galaxies. The next largest con- stituent is dark matter, which is an unknown form of matter. The rest of the universe consists of ordinary matter. Most of it is locked up in stars and clouds of gas. A tiny fraction of this matter is composed of heavier elements, the stuff of which humans and planets are made.' He would emphasise the word 'heavier', looking meaningfully at his listener. The success of this monologue inevitably varied.

Tuesday

Tuesday – Tin Box

You put me in a box
With a single biscuit crumb
As a beetle under glass
Lay toasting in the sun
You wound your troubles round me
A needle sewing dread
You let our love unravel
I might as well be dead.

Omega's mother looked slightly aghast at Tuesday's creation. She did like her poems to rhyme, but she hadn't quite foreseen where this particular poem was taking her. And there it was, the baldness of the word. *Dead.* The finality of it. And the way it snuck up on her. Presenting itself right at the end. Fitting in like a well-sewn snap fastener. Morbid. She started suddenly, as if she'd just heard a noise. *Morbid*, she thought again. She didn't feel quite so satisfied with this poem. And as she mused on this unfortunate turn of syntactic events, she turned the tin round and round in her hands, wondering how on earth that word had managed to insinuate itself again. At the same time the noise was getting louder, more insistent, so that the next moment she was jabbing violently at the smoke alarm with her sweeping brush, beating it into submission. And now she was sitting at the kitchen table, contemplating the charred remains of one very dead chocolate cake and wondering how Omega was doing, *sans* Cristelle.

It Might Never Happen

'It might never happen,' Mrs Gold was fond of saying. It was a piece of wisdom that Dawn had always found irritatingly ambiguous. Fine, she agreed, it might not, but then again it might. And what life had taught her (in her admittedly limited experience) is that it generally did. She called it Mum's Placebo Wisdom and although she wasn't entirely sure what she meant by this, she liked the sound of it and it made Mr Gold smile, which these days was a real rarity, even something of an event in its own small way. And Jack said, 'What's placebo?'

The Fat Lady has Sung

Twice.

Dawn's first love was José-Maria. And then, as far as she was concerned, he was also her last. He hadn't answered her e-mail. Not a single word in return. Inbox empty. Phone dead. Where had all the romance gone? She pictured a vast underground cavern stacked high with her exquisitely worded *belles-lettres*, emotions poured out in late night electronic correspondence, ardently whispered virtual phone calls. She realised that the cavern was full of unspoken words to José-Maria. That it exactly measured, in fact, the distance between them. And buried there, she pictured the wonderful lines of the letter she never sent and the admittedly less wonderful prose of the one she eventually did. But she didn't want to think about that now.

All gone to hell, she thought instead.

How Dawn's Parents See It (The Short History)

Torremolinos, late June 2006

Dear Mum and Dad,

Torremolinos is deadly. The girls are in great form. Jacintha's turned lobster red but she says it's got to be better than lily white. I'm not convinced. (Once she's happy.) Love to Jack.

xxxxxx Dawn

P.S. Met a nice boy called José-Maria from Madrid.

Torremolinos, late August 2006

Dear Mum and Dad,

Won't be home for the foreseeable future. José-Maria has proposed to me. He says he'll travel to Dublin in the spring to ask Dad for my hand in marriage. And Dad, don't act the eejit. Say 'YES!' Don't worry about school, I won't miss it and it won't miss me.

Lots of love
xxxxxxx Aurora

Madrid, early September 2006

Dear Mum and Dad,

Change of plan. See you Tuesday. Mum, can you pick me up at the airport? I'll be travelling alone.

Lots of love
Dawn

E-mail to Cristelle from Omega

Dublin, autumn 2006

Dear Cristelle,

The question of whether or not to plant trees outside our quiet suburban red-brick semi-detached homes has proved unexpectedly divisive. My mother is busy weaving her magic up and down the Villas seeking support from those who wish to maintain the status quo. After all, she points out, this is the way the Villas have looked for 100 years and why change now. Why indeed? I detect a certain Austenesque snobbism in conservative quarters, a reaction against the kind of *parvenu* or blow-in mentality of those who have been pressuring others to change.

This potential threat to the Villas' long-established ecosystem has revealed an impressively political side to my mother, who, if it weren't for the gravity of the situation, might be thought to be deriving great enjoyment from her status as sole conscientious objector.

In fact, word has it that generally very little thought was given to the possible pitfalls of such a programme, with the result that most reluctance was quashed by the heady enthusiasm of a few. After all, nobody likes to be seen to be going against what is perceived to be little short of a *fait accompli*.

The issue came to a head when we received a little note in our letterbox asking for our Yes Vote to trees in the Villas. It was, needless to mention, sent back as a terse NO and with it, but not in the same envelope, went another letter to the local authority ensuring we wouldn't be forced to have a tree outside our door if we didn't want one. A kind of totalitarian gloom was in the air, an all-in or all-out mentality that made my mother's intransigence seem almost heroic in the face of it. We heard stories of wavering and indecision followed by a gradual meltdown of defences and a signature that could potentially change the Villas' history forever.

Cries of parking problems and bird shit seemed to reawaken feeble opposition among those who had originally not given any great thought to the long-term implications of the proposal.

For the time being, the tree-lined avenue envisaged by the advocates of change remains a kind of personal dystopia. The local authority has promised not to disturb the section of century-old pavement outside our residence and our next-door neighbours have likewise opted for a treeless future.

No other news.

Missing you.

Come back soon.

I'm sorry.

Omega

P.S. I know you said you needed time, but three months seems a bit excessive to everyone I've discussed it with, including myself. And did you really need to put so many air miles between us? In all honesty I'm going nuts waiting for you. And nuts living in this empty flat. I found myself doing that daisy thing the other day. Petal after petal, she loves me, she loves me not. And then I realised I was investing my *whole being* in the last petal being a she-loves-me petal. And mercifully it was, or I would have been in for a really shit afternoon. Was the flower right?

P.P.S. How's Paris?

Mrs Gold, Feeling a Little Wistful

Wednesday – Untitled

Too swift to be a cloud
A plane moves across the sky
Payne's grey on pale grey
Lights blurred in rain
Where I am
Looking up
Muffled sounds surround
The silent image.

No dramatic contrasts here
But I imagine
That there's drama to be found
In the lives and loves of the
Sky-bound travellers
Leaving me behind
Feet on ground.

Life is Like an Onion

'Life is like an onion,' Omega's mother once told Cristelle. 'You peel off one layer at a time, and sometimes you weep.' Rose was peeling potatoes at the kitchen sink and Cristelle was crying because Omega had just broken up with her for the fifth time that year. Mrs Gold was very nice about it and said that her son was clearly an ingrate and didn't deserve her in the first place. Life seemed simpler back then.

Spiders and Flies

'What's Jack up to?' asked Dawn.

'Upstairs in his room. Probably playing with his marbles,' said Mrs Gold.

'Losing them, more like,' quipped Dawn.

'Possibly,' conceded Rose.

Jack was not playing with his marbles. He was manoeuvring a glass jar for better examination of its contents. The jar led a precarious existence perched on top of an upturned saucepan and crowned by a cork placemat. These carefully arranged items formed the bones of his laboratory.

'Jack's not right in the head.'

'Of course he is, Dawn! He just misses his mother. We all do.'

'But he's so unpredictable. One minute he can't stop talking and the next he's totally wrapped up in himself, capable of not uttering a single word for a week.'

'Just like his mother.'

Silence.

'Don't cry, Mum, please. I shouldn't have said anything.'

'That's all right, Dawn, I'm fine.'

E-mail from Cristelle to Omega

Paris, autumn 2006

Dear Omega,

I'm in Montmartre. From where I'm sitting, the Eiffel Tower looks skeletal in the distance, ghostly and strangely insubstantial.

The course is going well. I'm becoming a real expert. I've started looking at everything in terms of make-up. Pierre tells us we need to become *passionate* about colour, to *live* it, to *own* it...

He's very French.

But that is what I try to do. For example, when I look around me, I see Paris in autumn as a mix of dusky pinks and browns, greys shot through with cream and pale cerulean blues. And when I look at the people, I see two main categories. The first wear sombre blacks and greys, ivy greens, rusty oranges, smoky reds and purples; they are full of dark harmonious shades and tonalities. The others are like Jack's favourite cartoon characters, or escapees from a Toulouse Lautrec painting. They wear red and mustard scarves, felt hats and long charcoal grey overcoats. Bright colours, strong contrasts, wonderful fabrics.

Really, I can't stop thinking about cosmetics and clothes. When I look at the buildings – the eccentric black and white interior of the courtyard at the Palais Royal, or the curious multi-coloured mechanical fountains in the Centre Georges Pompidou – I try to imagine myself wrapping the colours and designs around me and what shade of lipstick might set it all off, what eyeliner or hair colour might work best. Whether it would *fonctionne*, as Pierre says.

The other day I went to visit the Sainte-Chapelle. I took the Métro to Cité and arrived at 9:30 only to find it didn't open until 10, so I went to a café and ordered a *café au lait, s'il vous plaît*, and read my guidebook. You would have laughed at the lofty descriptions: 'A reliquary chapel of the most daring gothic architecture,' it said, 'an airy cage of light to the holy relics', 'a jewel box'. It's always hard not to be disappointed with the real thing after reading guidebooks, don't you think? Like the first time you see the 'Mona Lisa', the real one, not the manipulated image you've been bombarded with all your life, and feel cheated because it's so bloody small. So ultimately *miss-able*. The waiter came over and saw what I was reading and he looked straight at me when handing me the bill, and said '*Vous allez à La Sainte-Chapelle, Mademoiselle?*' It was more of a statement than anything else, but I nodded politely and then he looked up towards the ceiling as if searching for the right words and finally at me again and said, as if he were imparting the secret of ever-lasting beauty, '*La Sainte-Chapelle, vous savez, c'est la couleur, la lumière, l'espace.*' It wasn't so much the words as the sheer intensity with which he pronounced them. He reminded me of Pierre in class when he looks like he's on the verge of weeping over Christian Dior's latest shade of lipstick.

So now I thought, it's all going to be downhill from here! But you know, the waiter wasn't wrong. The stained glass windows were truly incredible in the early morning light. I stood in the middle of the nave and just tried to absorb all the colours, to let them filter through me. I felt strangely light-headed all of a sudden. Like the first time we kissed. Do you remember?

And next thing I was crying because for some reason I found myself thinking about Hannah and the time she and I sat out on your front steps making necklaces and trading beads. We must have been very young. They were glass beads. Maybe that's why it came to mind.

And it was quite embarrassing because I couldn't stop weeping and all of a sudden this nice man in the Toulouse Lautrec style came over and said, *'Mademoiselle, ne pleurez pas. Je vous en prie! Ne pleurez pas!'* And he gave me a handkerchief, and stood there looking so genuinely distressed that I had to pull myself together, which I finally managed to do, before I thanked him and handed him back the by now sopping handkerchief.

It was one of those strange days that don't seem to fit in with any particular sequence of time or events.

Omega, I don't know when I'm coming home. I'm sorry, truly, for the note, and my subsequent 'disappearance', as you call it, even though if I'd wanted you not to know where I was going I wouldn't have been so stupid as to book my one-way flight to Paris on your Visa. The thing is, deep down, I think I wanted you to know where I had gone. But I couldn't face talking to you about it. Not after what happened.

Life after Jose-Maria

Dawn arrived home from Spain, pale but stoic.

Mr Gold sat waiting for her in the arrival hall; he'd been waiting for three hours. His mind pretended to be engrossed in his newspaper while his body acted as a kind of highly evolved fly-trapper, absorbing information from the air, mentally registering the flight data without consciously looking at it, listening to the announcements, sensing the growing restlessness of those who waited.

Finally.

We apologise for the late arrival of flight AZ-103 from Madrid. This flight has now landed.

Any minute now, he thought and settled back to reading.

Half an hour later, he became subliminally aware of fly-trapper signals and, glancing up, saw his daughter swing through the mirrored automatic doors.

'Dawn! Over here!' Dawn looked over and saw Henry

Gold a.k.a. Dad getting to his feet. She felt a sudden surge of love for this intensely familiar man.

Driving home, Mr Gold was delicate enough not to mention the second postcard. He decided on balance that there was no need for his daughter to know that he had absolutely no intention whatsoever of granting her hand in marriage to some oily Spaniard, to anyone at all for that matter – ever. He liked to think his refusal would have made a difference. But he knew he was deluding himself on that count. In truth, it was never his intention to *make any attempt to ever talk to* José-Maria, an attempt which would have been greatly facilitated by the fact they didn't speak the same language. He had long ago made up his mind to be no more an ambassador for Ireland in terms of charm and hospitality towards this oily Spaniard than a spider may be expected to welcome a fly into his web and never once think about eating him. Instead he said, 'Welcome home, Dawn.' And she replied, 'Thanks for coming to the airport' and continued to stare out the car window thinking about life after José-Maria and not for a moment being able to imagine how that life might be.

What's Jack Up To?

Jack of the hundred sandcastles, the thousand paper fish and boats, the million lost marbles, was asking his grandmother for the trillionth time, 'Where's Cristelle?' and Rose Gold was answering him as she had each time before, 'Cristelle is in Paris.'

'Why?'

'Because Cristelle and Omega have had a little argument and she's gone to Paris because she needs some time to think things out.'

Unexpectedly, Jack tried a new tactic. 'What things?'

'Things, Jack. Adult things.'

Mercifully, this seemed to work. But the respite was short-lived.

'Why?'

'Oh, Jack,' his grandmother said, 'I don't really understand it myself.'

Silence, finally.

Quo Vadis

When Dawn had been granted José-Maria-related compassionate leave from school for what seemed to Henry like a reasonable amount of time, he returned to the topic one morning over breakfast.

'So, Dawn,' Henry said, making a supreme effort to sound casual. 'Your mother and I were wondering...' Here he broke off, unsure of the optimal way to proceed.

Dawn was flicking impatiently through a copy of *Famous!* She glanced briefly at him before returning her attention to the perfect shiny lives depicted within.

'School,' Henry finally said, clinging to the only certainty available to him. 'You've missed just over a month now. When did we agree you'd go back?'

'We didn't,' said Dawn simply, picking up a half-eaten apple beside her cereal bowl and taking a monster bite. 'I've already told you,' she added. 'I'm not.'

Henry sighed and removed his spectacles, a sure sign he was losing ground.

'What about your Leaving Certificate?' he asked. 'Don't you feel it's a shame not to, well, see it through?'

'Nope,' replied Dawn cheerfully.

'Nothing we can do will change your mind?' Henry asked, though it was more of a statement than a question.

'Right again,' Dawn said, suddenly fascinated by the latest royal wedding on page 15.

'So what will you do?' Henry asked.

'Get a job,' Dawn said vaguely. 'Do some thinking.'

'Some thinking?'

'Yes, Dad,' Dawn replied in the tone she normally reserved for the terminally thick. 'Stock-taking, priorities, who am I, where did I come from, where am I going? You with me?'

Despite himself, Henry was.

Brooding

Thursday – Why?

Why do we wait so long
Wasted Minutes Hours and Days
Become the song of wasted dreams
The detritus of destinies.

Mrs Gold realised she had just written a poem that was a little bit about her and a little bit about Hannah and Dawn and a lot about Cristelle, who still hadn't come back from Paris, and wondered whether this 'poetry-writing lark', as Mr Gold was once fond of calling her daily ritual, was doing her any good. She decided to think about it tomorrow.

The Pub

'*Man's mind stretched to a new idea never goes back to its original dimensions.*' – Doubtfully attributed to Omega's mother by Omega's mother

Adam prepared to lower his third pint. But before he did, he thought he would just come out with it:

'Omega, what the hell happened with you and Cristelle?'

'I don't know. I grew up and became a bastard.'

'Try to be more specific.'

'I ignored the warning signs.'

'Great, that's great. Really specific.'

'You know, I let things slide, stopped paying attention, was always absorbed in my work.'

'Join the club.'

Silence.

'Okay, Omega, who did you sleep with?'

'No one! God! What kind of a bastard do you think I am?'

'Sure you want me to answer that?'

'No.'

'Okay, I won't.'

Silence, broken by Omega.

'Patricia.'

'Jesus, Omega, Patricia? Isn't she in Dawn's year at school? Was that *legal*?'

'I was so drunk, Adam, sooooo drunk. I can't bear to think about it. Cristelle had just hurled her wedding ring at me. She said she wanted a divorce. I thought it was over. Patricia came into the pub with a group of her mates. She came on to me…'

'Oh pull-ease,' said Adam. 'Don't give me that. It's the saddest, most pathetic line I've ever heard.'

'All right,' admitted Omega. 'Patricia was just…'

'What?' said Adam. 'There?'

Omega winced.

'No, no… She was, it was…'

'The suicide jump?' Adam ventured.

'Something I will never forgive myself for,' said Omega quietly.

'Does Dawn know?'

'Yes, says she hopes we both have a nice comfortable journey to hell.'

'So what are you going to do?'

'Pray.'

'You're an atheist, Omega.'

'So? I got married in a church.'

'Is that relevant?'

'Does it have to be?'

'Oh right, sorry, I didn't realise I was having a conversation with your feminine side. So, how was it?'

'I can't remember.'

'Jesus, Omega! I mean telling Cristelle.'

'I didn't tell her. She took one look at me when I got home, extracted a confession, and the next day she was gone.'

The E-mail Dawn Sent

Dublin, early October 2006

Dear José-Maria,

Congratulations. You've ruined my life.

Dawn

Henry Gold

Henry Gold worked in the Natural History Museum. He would arrive punctually every day, Monday to Friday, and take up his station near the door, 10 a.m. to 5 p.m.

Henry Gold: Custodian of dead things. Since 1976.

The first time he saw Rose, she was nineteen years old. She was standing in front of a whale's skeleton, thinking about the clammy weight of mortality in its bones and about the poem she would write down later, entitled 'The Clammy Weight of Mortality', and he was on the other side of the large hall, so that she appeared to him to be a glorious hybrid of everything that was most precious to him in the world. Obscured here and there by the whale's ancient bones, she was a perfect symbiosis of the living and the dead, the animal and organic. She was wearing a long green wool coat and carrying a tapered yellow umbrella in her left hand. Her hair fell down her back almost to her waist, unhampered by clips or bows or strings. Her features were dainty; her nose, mouth and eyes all carefully arranged in neat, linear proportions. She was positively aglow with youth and vitality. Henry Gold took one look at her and he never, ever looked back.

In the heady days of their courtship, they would often stroll down Dún Laoghaire pier at night, pausing to buy a Teddy's ice cream or steal a kiss under her yellow umbrella in the rain. They would spend hours talking about poetry and insects and destiny.

Over time the abstract gave way to more concrete notions of marriage, children and a shared future. And Henry always thinks it was natural that this should happen, but also sad somehow.

Hannah was Henry and Rose's first born. She was like Rose in looks and Henry in temperament. When she was seventeen she came home one evening and told them she was pregnant, and that she was sorry. Jack's origins were never revealed and nobody asked any questions. Not that they didn't speculate, being human, but Hannah didn't want to tell and that was that.

And of course, after the car crash, that was definitively that.

These thoughts filtered in and out of Henry Gold's fly-trapper mind as he sat in the Natural History Museum. He found that increasingly it was to Hannah his thoughts turned and he wondered if her departure was not the point when, for the first time, almost imperceptibly, he began to move away from Rose – or was it her from him? It was so hard to tell. Henry would be the first to admit that he was not the world's most loquacious man, but in recent times he had surpassed even his own expectations of what was possible in terms of economising on the spoken word, retreating into what was basically an uninterrupted silence.

To his dismay, even the insects and dead animals, which for so long were a source of never-ending amazement and joy, had ceased to command his attention in the way they once did. The glass covers of the display cases revealed themselves to him as being nothing but the receptacles of minute dust particles.

Particles so small that they were all but invisible to the human eye, but nonetheless there they were. On one case lingered the ghostly smudge of an overenthusiastic child who jabbed the glass with a podgy index finger, pointing to one or other of the winged still lives. And Henry, normally such a zealot when it came to wiping away digital imprints, had left it there.

The truth is that he had never really even begun to get over Hannah's death. And Rose told him it had been four years – that she couldn't bear to see him like this, that Omega felt neglected by him and unloved, that Dawn was mixed-up and upset about the 'oily Spaniard' and that little Jack was confused, God-love-him, and that she herself missed him and for-God's-sake SAY SOMETHING!

Henry shifted in his seat.

Friday

(The day after Dawn announced *almost casually* that she may be pregnant and Omega hinted at why there was a very good chance Cristelle was never coming back from Paris.)

<u>Friday – Untitled</u>

You weigh a tonne
I'm a balloon
Caught in your spoke
On a hot afternoon.

Her first thought of the day rhymed, so Rose thought she might as well write it down as her daily poem. She knew that if she didn't seize on it right away, the chance was that she would think of nothing else to write down that day: in terms of poetry.

Jack

Jack was sitting in Dawn's room, humming. He was wearing one of her letters on his head, and around him he saw to his satisfaction that there were at least twenty more hats, a similar number of boats and many, many fish. He thought he would bring them downstairs soon, to show Gran.

E-mail to Cristelle from Omega

Dublin, autumn 2006

Dear Cristelle,

All hell broke lose back at the ranch yesterday when Dawn came home to find Mum in the kitchen ironing her letters! It seems Jack has now mastered the Japanese art of origami with a skill and dexterity (except for the fish) that left all of us – Dawn especially – speechless. With the boats and hats it wasn't so bad because the basic shape is rectangular. But for the fish Jack had folded the A4 pages into a square and torn off the superfluous rectangle, sometimes neatly enough, but mostly making a hash of it so the fish looked more like mutant tadpoles than anything else. The point, of course, is that he'd severed off bits of Dawn's letters and strewn them around the room, these extra bits not being needed for the execution of his master plan: to succeed in turning practically every letter Dawn has ever written into something that you either put on your head or in water.

By the time the little origami master was apprehended, he had practically covered the entire period of Dawn's I-DON'T-WANT-TO-TALK-ABOUT-IT

Spanish romance and in the face of Jack's paper-folding activities even Dad was uncharacteristically moved to utterance, remarking that Jack must be tossing up a future career as milliner or mariner. Everybody laughed except Dawn and Jack.

I can't bear the thought of going into work tomorrow. It's really beginning to get to me. The old bastard just sits in his office all day like some sort of maleficent Buddha, perched in the middle of all his tinny plaques and fake papyrus scrolls as if they mean something to anyone with half a brain and I keep waiting to spot the lotus petals emerging from his ass or see him levitating just above them, like the poxy little Buddha he is.

He called me into the office the other day and said he felt I was on the right track, going in the right direction. I mean what am I? The 18:00 Eurostar to Paris?

I went back to my desk and thought about transforming the plans I've been working on into a perfectly formed miniature origami zoo à la Jack and depositing the whole ark on his shiny walnut desk with a little accompanying note saying, 'Be good to the other animals, I won't be back,' but then I thought the whole significance would probably be entirely lost on him and this thought was so depressing that I just sidled off home instead, like the stinking coward I am.

Meanwhile, Adam is going around with an unbearably smug expression on his face because he's managed to get the Taoiseach on board for the opening. Big deal. Adam says I'm the one who's unbearable these days. Last night he refused to come to the pub with me. He said he couldn't cope being around all this unhappiness. He suggested I write to you instead, try and sort things out. But here I am, talking about work, the thing that pulled us apart in the first place. And…god, Cristelle, I was catatonic. I know you don't want to believe me or forgive me or can't, but it's the truth. And I genuinely thought it was all over with us. You had just hurled your wedding ring at me, remember?

Please tell me we can work this out.

Omega

José-Maria

So I got this e-mail saying 'Congratulations. You've ruined my life' and you tell me, what Z-Ell is a man supposed to do?

Dawn

'Negative.'

'Negative, you're absolutely 100 per cent sure about that that?'

'Positive.'

'*What?*'

'I'm positive it's negative! You're in the clear, home free, saved.'

'Oh thank God. THANK-YOU-GOD!'

The Teeth Dream (Again)

Rose just had the teeth dream again. It always started the same way. She was about to eat something, usually an apple (once it was a stick of celery), only to realise she couldn't because she hadn't got any teeth. Funnily enough, in the dream this never caused her any great distress. What she experienced was more a feeling of vague surprise. *Oh*, she always thought, *how am I going to eat the apple now?* It was afterwards, when she woke up, that she was assailed by a moment of sheer terror. She lay there, petrified. Eventually, she plucked up the courage to swallow, and as she did, realised she had just champed down on her molars. And then utter relief poured through every limb in her body until finally she could say to herself *just the teeth dream again, Rose. Go back to sleep.* But this time she couldn't go back to sleep. She lay awake thinking of how Dawn once told her that she read somewhere that teeth dreams are metaphors, metaphors about the dreamer's relationship with their house, about all their repressed fears for its occupants.

She got up and went down to the kitchen. Sitting down, she half thought she might write a poem, but nothing, absolutely nothing, came to mind. Instead she cast her eye over the neatly aligned notebooks that now covered five shelves, almost thirty years of marriage to Henry and over twenty-six of mother-hood to Hannah, Omega and Dawn, and taking down a notebook at random, read to herself in the early morning light. She read the poem she wrote after her first date with Henry. They had spent the morning in the Natural History Museum. Henry was glowing. The thought never once struck him that this girl might think him odd to want to go to his place of work on a Sunday morning, and in reality the thought never did strike Rose, so it was a merciful omission on both their part.

They started out on the ground floor, making their way past the massive skeleton of the giant Irish deer. A group of children were clustered around it, listening to their tour guide with varying degrees of concentration. He was trying to explain the concept of 37,000 years ago. 'Who is the oldest person you know?' the guide inquired, looking from one to the other. 'God,' said a small boy promptly. Next he tried explaining that the deer's antlers weighed 800 to 900 kilos. 'How heavy do you think that is?' he asked his diminutive public. 'As heavy as a TV?' ventured a small girl with pig-tails. The group now stood surveying the otters. 'Can you eat them?' demanded one of the children. 'Is there a unicorn?' someone else wanted to know. Henry and Rose smiled at each other and moved on.

They looked at the golden eagle. Rose imagined how graceful it must be in flight. They laughed at the pygmy shrew and the bloated puffer fish with its glassy stare. They stood respectfully in front of a basking shark, the second biggest of its species in the world.

They spent a long time at Table Case 28: Irish Marine Shells. Rose was amazed at the sheer variety of forms and colours. She especially loved their double-barrelled names. There were Venus clams, sunset shells, sea butterflies, dog cockles, saddle oysters, Pandora's boxes. Her eyes darted from one to the other. Henry stood beside her, the happiest man in Dublin.

Next, he brought her on a grand tour of the insect world. Rose had never imagined that anyone could know so much about these little creatures, and communicate their knowledge with such passion. In one of the cases, there were short biographies of famous Irish naturalists complete with newspaper clippings and old black and white photographs. Rose noted the interests of one James Nathaniel Halbert, M.C.I.A. (1872–1948): 'beetles, true-bugs, lacewings, caddis-flies, dragonflies, damselflies, stoneflies and water-mites.' Among the many achievements of Prof. George Herbert Carpenter (1865–1939) was 'the solving of the problem of that highly injurious insect, the Warble Fly.' Rose had never even heard of a warble fly, let alone of any problem related to its existence. She was amazed and amused to learn that insects were an 'Irish Success Story'. A little note explained why: 'Insects are very successful and they outnumber in species all the other animals. They usually only come to the attention of most people by accident. Nevertheless, they have fascinated many men and women.' Rose *was* fascinated. She really was.

On the first floor, she resisted an irrational impulse to hug the giant polar bear. On the second, she laughed out loud at the Latin name for the long-tongued fruit bat: the *macroglossus minimus*. On the third, she lingered in front of the bee hummingbird, trying to imagine what it would be like to actually see a bird fly backwards. She hadn't known that any could. She pondered over the meaning of the fin whale's status: *vulnerable* said the index card. How could something that measured 19.8 metres be vulnerable? She thought about what the people in Bantry Bay must have thought back in 1862 when this gigantic corpse floundered on their shore.

On floor four she recoiled from the giant edible crab's enormous pincers. 'Meaning *we* eat it?' she asked Henry nervously.

What pleased her most, though, were Leopold and his son Rudolph Blaschka's exquisite glass models of marine life. Henry told her that the collection was

quite possibly the museum's most precious possession: an inspired purchase way back when the
Blaschka family, who originated in Venice, had
applied their knowledge of decorative glass to the
construction of these incredibly detailed specimens.
Natural history museums and aquaria around the
world commissioned their work, unrivalled for its
superb craftsmanship and beauty. There were replicas
of jellyfish, starfish, squid and molluscs, each one a
masterpiece in its own right. The Blaschkas were so
famous, Henry said, that they even had their own
entry in the Encyclopaedia Britannia, under
'Blaschka glass'.

She lingered over the table cases, reluctant to leave.

When they finally did, it was drizzling rain and
Henry held her yellow umbrella above them both as
they made their way across the leaf-strewn lawn
outside. They walked past Greene's bookstore, skirted
the iron railings of Trinity College into
Westmoreland Street and into Bewley's for coffee and
a cherry bun. They sat facing the stained glass
windows and when Rose looked at the myriad of
insects depicted between the lead panelled panes of
glass, she felt like she was seeing them for the first
time. 'Harry Clarke,' Henry told her, when he saw her

staring at them. 'A genius.' Later they strolled up Grafton Street, pausing here and there to look at the shop window displays. They ended up in Stephen's Green. And this is what Rose remembered best. Not the rest of the day – the details of Henry's discourses had long since faded from memory. No. What Rose remembered was sitting in Stephen's Green with Henry on Saturday afternoon in 1977.

Saturday (1977)

Tentative, as always
First you crafted a tiny bridge
For my paper boats to sail under
You threw it my way
Like a magician throwing
Cards on a table

And it seemed to me that the space
     between us
Was the arched curve of this bridge
And you traced its lines for me
With your body.

I was cross-legged, in the act
Of remembering
Things that don't include you
Contemplative.

71

You may have felt a strange urge to reach
*   me then*
To anchor me somehow
Before the tide came in
I hope that's what you felt.

And we sat there for
The longest time
Silent
Your head in my lap
And the tiny bridge
You built
Between us.

Rose sat in the kitchen, the notebook open in her lap, and when she finally glanced up she saw Henry standing framed in the kitchen door, watching her.

'Henry,' she said suddenly, frowning involuntarily, before she could stop herself, 'when did the bridge collapse?' The edges around the words were rough. She hadn't meant to sound so cutting. He continued to gaze at her from the kitchen door and for a second she thought perhaps the question had never actually passed her lips. That she had only imagined herself saying it out loud.

But Henry had heard.

'I think,' he said finally, pausing in mid-sentence, 'when I realised I wasn't a very good architect.'

Henry turned and padded out of the kitchen in his soft checked slippers as soundlessly as he had come in. Rose continued to sit alone at the table. The clock seemed to tick louder.

Rose Gold, she thought with sudden uncharacteristic bitterness, *a lifetime of letting other people get on the bus first*.

The thought, like her poems, came from nowhere.

Marble Halls

Henry used to call Hannah 'my bohemian girl' in homage to her unconventional dress sense and outlook on life, but especially, and most memorably, to her performance of Balfe's oneiric masterpiece when she was 17 years old. It was the final year concert. Hannah was upset because she had been passed over for the valedictory, which was delivered instead by Maria. There was no doubt in anyone's mind but Hannah's that her true talent lay in singing. Not that she wasn't good at writing too. She was. But the teachers' laudable sense of justice decreed that Maria should give the farewell speech and Hannah should do what she was born to do: sing.

Maria's speech was witty and unusually mature for a girl of her age. Rose leaned over and smiled graciously at Maria's mother. Like any parent, she had been disappointed for Hannah's sake. But she also knew the teachers were right. Her daughter's voice was what made her stand out.

As the applause died away, Hannah got up reluctantly from her seat and walked slowly and somewhat heavily to the stage. Mr O'Donovan, the music teacher, gave her the note.

She cleared her throat and looked around her nervously.

'I dreamt,' she began, but her voice cracked with nerves. The strain of the performance in front of the entire school was evidently proving too much.

Rose looked at her daughter.

Come on, she willed silently. *You know you can do it.* Hannah gulped and looked in her parents' direction.

A few people coughed in the audience. A group of girls started giggling and Rose glared at them over her glasses.

Then something happened on the stage. Hannah seemed to draw herself up to her full height – no mean feat, given she was just a little over five feet five inches. She pursed her lips and closed her eyes. Rose knew she was mentally battling her demons. Standing there, she looked almost angry.

Her music teacher glanced over solicitously. He played the chords again, softly, unhurriedly.

Hannah inhaled.

When she exhaled, it was pitch perfect.

I dreamt I dwelt in marble halls,
With vassals and serfs at my side, sang Hannah.
And of all who assembled within those walls,
That I was the hope and the pride...
I had riches too great to count
Could boast of a high ancestral name;

There you go, thought Rose. *You're flying now.*

But I also dreamt, which pleased me most, Hannah continued, a tiny tremor in her voice,
That you lov'd me still the same
That you lov'd me, you lov'd me still the same,
That you lov'd me, you lov'd me still the same.

Rose had the strongest impression that these last lines were sung directly at her and Henry, who confirmed Rose's intuition by raising his eyebrows questioningly at her.

When Hannah stopped singing, the room erupted into sincere, sustained applause.

That was the night Hannah told her parents she was pregnant.

Afterwards, in her saddest moments, Rose thought of Hannah alone on the stage. Her songbird, her nightingale. How frightened yet fierce she'd been.

Thursday: Your Tomb Unmade

The page is blank
The ink run dry
The die is cast
My butterfly
My nightingale
My heart's dear song
My swollen womb
My papillon
You were too young
Your tomb unmade
Would it were I
In your shallow grave
The water swirls
About my pen
Your voice returns
Indelible.

There is no getting over death, Rose reflected. Only, perhaps, a moving beyond or past it – to another place entirely. The journey, once made, changes you utterly. You will not recognise yourself when you arrive at your destination.

The Golden Tulip

The handkerchief-bearer looked searchingly at the willowy girl sitting opposite him, nervously twisting his once pristine square of pure cotton in her hands. He'd had to insist, of course. She had more need of it than him. It gave him pleasure to give it to her. An unlikely souvenir of the Sainte-Chapelle, etc., said with just the right amount of self-deprecating charm. She rewarded him with a wide-eyed smile: a field of sunflowers turning in unison to face the sun. It took his breath away, that smile, the sheer unexpectedness of it in the middle of all those tears. And he had to fight really hard not to give in to the terrifying impulse that threatened to overcome him at any moment, telling him to drop to his knees and make a total, unmitigated fool of himself. Instead, he said, 'English?' and she shook her head. 'No, Irish.'

His name was Luc and he was staying in the Golden Tulip nearby and would she care to join him for a coffee, and incredibly she said yes, and this was what they were doing now, just as Omega was peering gloomily over the brim of his fifth Guinness in Dublin. With Adam looking gloomily back.

The Palace Bar

'*Flamma fumo est proxima*,' announced Adam, in a desperate attempt at defusing the dreary atmosphere. He winked feebly at Omega over the bar menu.

'You what?' said Omega glumly. (Adam's predilection for Latin maxims was one of his less endearing traits.)

'Where there is smoke, there is fire, my dear Omega,' said Adam, grinning broadly at his own erudition. Omega merely grunted, then glanced up over the bar and was inspired by a little sign on the wall. He looked back at Adam sitting opposite him and sentenced: 'Be good or be gone.'

Another Knock at the Door

Dawn opened it.

José-Maria appeared before her. Suitcase in hand.

Dawn snapped her eyes shut.

She waited for what seemed like an eternity.

Opened them again.

Incredible. He was still there. Undeterred. Smiling. Grinning, even.

Dawn froze.

In retrospect, she had to admit that for once, Jack was on cue. She hadn't seen him creep up behind her, his voice emerging from somewhere under her left armpit, tugging at her sleeve.

'Dawn, Dawn, is that the oily Spaniard?'

A Foot in the Door

Dawn attempted to slam the front door shut. José-Maria inserted the tip of his silver runner just in time.

'What are you, *loco*?' he shouted at her. 'I come all the way here to explain things and you bang the door in my face?'

'If that's what it takes,' Dawn retorted.

'Crazy *and* stupid?' he asked in a gentler tone, looking deep into her eyes. She shoved the door again but with less conviction.

'Look,' said José-Maria, 'when I told you to buy a one-way ticket home for Christmas, I didn't really mean it!'

'It sure didn't sound that way,' snarled Dawn.

'I didn't! It wasn't really me talking,' insisted José-Maria, looking suddenly abashed.

'Oh, hello?' said Dawn, in the voice she reserved for people scoring way beneath the contempt level. 'So who was it then? Your evil twin? The other half of your split personality?'

'No, no! Nothing like that,' said José-Maria, looking more miserable by the minute. Dawn went to close the door.

'It was my mother,' he whispered, staring at his shoes.

This explanation was so unexpected that she took a step backwards, inadvertently opening the door wider. José-Maria attempted to get his other foot in.

'You mean to tell me,' Dawn said, placing her hands on her hips for special effect, 'that we broke up because *your mother* didn't approve of me?'

José-Maria mumbled something under his breath. Dawn put her right hand up to her ear and made a face. 'What?'

'She expressed some reservations when you got to Madrid,' José-Maria said in a tiny whisper.

'Some reservations?' asked Dawn, incredulous, her right eyebrow shooting up.

'She said I was breaking her heart, by being with the Irish.'

'*The Irish?*' Dawn repeated, blinking rapidly. 'What, like she thought you were with all of us?'

Now it was José-Maria's turn to look puzzled. 'What?' he asked.

'Never mind,' snapped Dawn. 'Tell me why you didn't answer my e-mail.'

'I wanted to,' José-Maria replied. Dawn looked him over for a long time.

'I'm extremely mad at you,' she said, finally. José-Maria continued to look at his shoes. Rose appeared at the doorway and smiled warmly at the visitor, then looked questioningly at Dawn.

'In or out?' she enquired pleasantly. She could have been talking about three-quarter length versus the mini.

'In,' growled Dawn, 'by a neck.'

Rose Gold

Rose Gold was twitching on her seat. She just couldn't get comfortable. She kept glancing at her watch, then at her bag, then at the passenger in the seat beside her. He seemed unbearably calm. The epitome of serene. If he were being marketed, they'd call him *totally zen*. She examined his facial muscles for tell-tale clenching. Nothing. Not even a glitch. The man reminded her of this religious statue she had once seen on a travel programme, some obscure Hindu deity. She was so intent on this comparison that she gave a little start when the deity leaned towards her conspiratorially and said, 'You okay? You look kind of freaked.' And smiled a most disconcerting grin. *Big teeth*, she registered, and careful not to verbalise, replied, 'Oh, yes, thank you, I'm fine. I mean, I'm...you're right, nervous. It's just that I've never travelled alone before, well, flown alone, that is, and it's, well, I'm...not used to it,' she concluded lamely. Much to her surprise, her answer seemed to meet with Totally Zen's total approval. The man just nodded, still grinning, and said, 'No sweat, do it once, you'll never look back.' Then he leaned back in his seat and half-closed his eyes, his body language telling her this conversation was over. He meant to sound comforting, she knew. But she couldn't help feeling that he was overestimating her ability to be soothed by the kind of trite banality he had just lobbed her way. Totally Zen's quick-fix mechanics for troubled souls. She examined him again. He was looking and acting less like a Hindu deity by the minute. More like one of those cheesy American gurus on pay TV, the ones that talked about simplifying your life in five easy steps and then asked you for a credit card donation. She caught the air hostess's eye. The girl flashed her an automatic nanosecond smile. The world, Rose reflected, was one big fake, and quite inexplicably began to feel better.

The Great Hall of Evolution

'After a walk among elephants, giraffes, butterflies, moose, leatherback turtle, albatross…the visitor thinks about unity and evolution of life.'

Cristelle was actually thinking about Henry Gold in Dublin and how much he would have loved to see this gallery, how he would have marvelled at its wide open spaces, its glass arches, the breathtaking modernity of it all. He would have especially liked, she thought, the Gallery of Entomology and the Menagerie. She lingered by a collection of goldfish, *carassius auratus*, swimming unperturbed in their glassy environs. Their colours reminded her a little of the latest Gaultier collection; she noted an interesting combination of mascarpone and cassis. They weren't unlike those glass Murano sweets she once bought for Omega's mother in Venice. Jack had tried to eat one and nearly choked on it. It was terrible.

They'd had to rush him off for an emergency stomach pump. It turned out that he had actually spat it out but was enjoying the attention too much to tell anyone. It must have been almost a year after the car accident, she mused. January, maybe? There was a little sign beside the fish informing the visitors that the domestication of the *'poissons rouges'* dated from the eighteenth century in China, but they had been subject to breeding since the twelfth century. Thanks to the efforts of these breeders, the sign said smugly, nowadays there were some 200 different species. It all seemed very self-congratulatory. Man's great triumph over the goldfish. Preserved for Chinese restaurants worldwide. She watched a small black fish dart in and out of the feathery aquatic plants that furnished the pebble-strewn bottom of the aquarium. It was entirely black except for one brilliant streak of orange that cut diagonally across its body, glinting as it passed. *That would be Omega,* she thought grimly. *The black fish of the family.* She saw another one, brightly coloured, a cocktail of pink and yellow. Dawn. She was just looking for Henry and Rose when Luc came over and whispered something about getting a coffee. Cristelle could never understand why people whispered in museums. Maybe it was out of some sort of weird respect for dead animals. Still, she was grateful to leave them behind. She was beginning to obsess again. As she turned to go, she noticed the black fish had swum right up to the edge of the glass, and was kind of head butting it, his glassy eyes staring at her with what could only be described as a reproachful kind of glare. She shook her head rapidly and blinked him out of her line of sight, then flashed Luc – who was looking at her kind of strangely – a reassuring smile and squeezed his arm lightly. 'Let's take a walk in the gardens,' she suggested. 'And then go for tea in the mosque across the road.'

Luc, who would have taken her for tea to China if she had asked him, acquiesced.

Lost Shoes

Rose was walking across an ornamental wooden bridge with a brilliant vermilion lacquered finish. On waking, she would observe that she had somehow managed to wander straight into one of her Japanese prints hanging in the downstairs hallway. In the distance, she could just make out the silhouette of a tiny Buddhist temple, shimmering in the mist. She was nibbling on a lotus fruit in a state of dreamy languor. A soft breeze caressed her face and hair, carrying with it the softest tinkling of bells imaginable. She had almost reached the other side when she glanced down at her feet and realised she was wearing no shoes. Puzzled, she retraced her steps and, sure enough, there were her soft silk slippers with intricate coloured beadwork and embroidered animal motifs resting neatly side by side on the ground. She bent to retrieve them, and sighing as she put them on, started to walk back over the bridge. But just as she was approaching the exact same spot as before, she looked down and realised the slippers had vanished again. Feeling slightly exasperated now, she retreated and found them back where they'd started. She took her time putting them on, twirling first her right, then her left foot in turn, and satisfied they were securely attached, made her way for the third time across the bridge. As she walked, she stared intently at her errant slippers. The only way she could describe it afterwards was that every step she took, the shoes seemed to recede from her feet, like slowly melting ice cream. It happened so gradually that she kept blinking to make sure they were really disappearing. As the last glimmer of silk faded into nothing, she stopped, staring incredulously at her bare feet. When Rose described the dream to Dawn, her daughter's response was, 'So leave the shoes and cross anyway.' It hadn't even occurred to Rose as a possibility.

Luc Lamure

Luc worked as a financial analyst for one of the big banks in Paris. He was into 'empowerment' and 'soft skills', 'best practices' and 'new order economies'. He read the financial papers voluntarily. He tracked the markets in much the same way as the astrologers would have charted the constellations. For reasons that were not immediately obvious, he also dabbled in *I Ching* and the esoteric arts. For a while, he had attended a yoga class, but he stopped going when the advances of one of the male participants began to make him question his sexuality. He was thirty-five years old.

Later, when they were sipping sweet mint tea from tiny green glasses in the mosque and eating strange almond cakes that seemed to be covered in birdseed, he told Cristelle that it was highly significant they should have met in the Sainte-Chapelle.

She looked at him blankly, but not discouragingly.

They had met under the Rose Window, he said, which depicted what?

He had this vaguely annoying habit of asking questions that invariably only he was in a position to answer.

'What?' Cristelle dutifully supplied.

'The Apocalypse,' he said, looking at her intensely.

Cristelle felt a little under pressure. 'Oh,' she said, raising her eyebrows. 'Right.'

He waved her guidebook at her.

'Listen!' he said. 'Listen to what it says.'

She felt mildly annoyed at the proprietary way he was handling her guidebook and made a mental note to be the first to pick it up when they were leaving.

Luc leaned back in his chair, placing the book on the table in front of him, and intoned, 'NOTE: In the centre, Christ is surrounded by seven golden candelabra, he is dressed in a violet cloak and white robes and is seated on a rainbow, a blade covers his mouth and seven stars shoot over from his right hand onto a blue background.'

'What do you think it means?' she asked, feeling the first flicker of genuine curiosity.

'I have no idea,' said Luc, not missing a beat. 'But I feel sure it's quite significant.'

E-mail to Omega from Cristelle

Paris, autumn 2006

Dear Omega,

I'm worried about your mother. I get this awful feeling she's on some kind of mission to save the world. You don't think she's going to try and 'save our marriage' or anything mad like that, do you? I got this postcard from her the other day and it was more than usually cryptic. The part where you normally write was blank and on the front there was this black and white photo of John Lennon on a bicycle with Yoko Ono standing behind him. And when I looked again at the blank part I realised that it wasn't actually entirely empty. It had some kind of tiny winged insect on it that I think she must have drawn herself. And beside it – it was barely legible – she'd written 'peace'. I mean, is she okay?

Love,

Cristelle

Water

Dublin, autumn 2006

Dear Cristelle,

Lately I've been having the most awful dreams. I'm practically dredging up pre-natal memories at this point, I've gone way beyond stage one and two; these are bona fide level three dreams. They're so realistic that when I wake up I feel like that Chinese man who dreamed he was a butterfly and on waking, couldn't decide whether he was in fact a butterfly, dreaming that he was a man, or a man dreaming he was a butterfly. My dreams have this febrile kind of intensity, an organic magic mushroom experience. Everything is zooked to the point of hyper-real. The colours are blindingly sharp, the outlines clearer than

DVD. The sounds have a crystalline quality. In one dream I'm sitting at this bright red plastic table on a canary yellow chair in a small bar. The bar is painted a kind of El Greco lime green, and there's an old-fashioned jukebox in the corner playing Elvis. It's not clear where I am or what time it is. The street outside is empty. The bar is dimly lit. At a certain point I realise that outside it's raining. The drops start off small, almost invisible. They patter on the pane. It's a soothing kind of sound, like being in a Japanese water garden. Then they start getting louder and bigger. Huge, watery drops. But it's strange. Because I notice that just beyond the footpath the sun is shining really brightly and the pavement is completely dry. So I tilt my head and look upwards and see this one enormous inky grey cloud sitting directly over the bar. And meanwhile the drops just get bigger and bigger, and now they are hurling themselves against the window with a deafening crash, and I start worrying that the glass is going to break at any moment. They're literally flinging themselves at it in a kind of frenzy.

Then I begin to see that they are not just made of water, there are all kinds of strange objects inside them. One particularly enormous one contains an elephant. But there are smaller ones too, with photos inside, an old comb, a light bulb, a tiny one with a toothpick, there's even one containing a key. But what really captures my attention is the one that smashes open, leaving a photo stuck to the glass. It kind of hangs there for a while, before it starts sliding down. It's a picture of us at our wedding. There you are, looking dazzling in that dress you wore, and there I am, except instead of it being me there's a pig-man in a suit. You've got my trotter in your hand. I've got a curly tail peeping out from behind my jacket. I'm inside the café staring at this thing and I suddenly start to bawl. And very quickly my feet are in puddles of tears, and the water inside and outside is rising. And next thing I'm floating upwards and desperately trying to keep my head above the water. I'm totally panicking. But even while I'm panicking, I begin to feel a bizarre kind of calm settle over me. I even think, what the hell, I've always wanted to see what it was like to die. And just as I think that, I wake up and I'm at home and my pillow is sopping because I've knocked over the bottle of water on my bedside table and my cheeks are wet because I've been crying in my sleep. And I think that this is not going to be a very good day.

Do you think I need therapy?

Love,

Omega

E-mail to Dawn from Cristelle

Paris, autumn 2006

Dear Dawn,

There are a few things that I just don't get about
Parisian women. Chief among these is their enduring
love affair with the ballerina shoe. Especially popular
this autumn are the metallic variations on the theme:
the dainty feet of almost every third woman I see are
encased in gold, silver or bronze slippers. The little
pieds dart past like a shoal of iridescent fish, flashing
down the steps to the Métro, darting into Zara or
peeking out from under the tables of the sidewalk
cafés.

What is it exactly that gives with this shoe? Is Degas
to blame? Years of exposure to those innumerable ballerinas in the Musée d'Orsay, bending gracefully over
their satin ribbons? Or does it run deeper? Has it to do
with the psyche of the quintessentially French
woman? Small is beautiful. Petite is beautiful. Flat is
beautiful. I can't work it out. Honestly, the amount of
ballerinas on the streets here is mind-blowing. It's like
this one-shoe-fits-all mentality writ large. And while

I'm on this theme, what is it with the particularly French female obsession with all things small and cute? Even my accent is a '*petite accente Irlandaise*.' The Irish part I get, but what on earth is so bloody small about it? Why can't it just be an Irish accent? Why does it have to be cute? Another thing – go figure – is the French woman's almost total disdain for make-up and hair dye. How on earth, I'm thinking, do cosmetic companies survive here? You see these women all the time, fabulously dressed, immaculately turned out, but zero make-up. Lipstick, especially, is almost totally unheard of on Parisian streets. Believe me, I've been looking. I mean, is their idea of canonic beauty really the pinched moue of Juliette Binoche, pert nose wrinkled, a little frown just above the mascara-less eyelashes, a body that's barely on the right side of anorexic? The more anaemic and drained looking, the better. Go eat a steak, I'm thinking, and live a little – put on some heels!

Well, these are my thoughts of the day! How are you? Have you heard anything from your Spanish man?

Cristelle

Natural History Museum

'The opening of the Natural History Museum in 1857 was marked by a lecture on recent "African Discoveries" by Dr David Livingstone. The impression today is that not much has changed in the museum since then, for it retains a certain olde world charm and plenty of Victorian clutter. Indeed, anyone seeking to find out how "the past" was presented in the last century would do well to check out the archaic displays and the quirky language used to describe the exhibits. Visitors to the ground floor can see specimens of Irish wildlife and fauna, while upstairs, all manner of preserved beasts attest to the skill of the taxidermists of old. Other exhibits, including two whales suspended from the roof, have been reduced to their skeletal cores, which makes for fascinating viewing, particularly for children. The museum is also a research centre, which specialises in the study of insects. Excited entomologists can be seen scurrying through its corridors – the museum's collection of creepy crawlies is said to run to some 500,000.'

Rain, Hail or Shine

Henry Gold opened his eyes and observed that he was feeling a little disoriented. He had taken the 8:05 train from Booterstown, as always. He had waited patiently on the platform, coat folded loosely over his left arm, newspaper tightly rolled and tucked like a giant paper thermometer under his right armpit, right hand extended a little awkwardly at a right angle in an attempt not to drop the paper, briefcase and umbrella held aloft. The grey shadow of the approaching train had raced into the station, nose to nose with its green doppelganger, yellow headlights glinting feral and owl-like in the bright autumn sun. A startled bird flew up as it raced past, its wings scattering the surrounding silence. From a distance, the train evoked the roar of the incoming tide, but as it moved closer, the noise broke up into its constituent mechanical parts. The pavement below Henry's feet was littered with cigarette butts and off-white chewing gum. Oddly artificial-looking moss clung to the winding cracks of the flagstones, suggesting a fierce struggle for life below. Henry observed these stubborn life forms with mild detached interest, sorting and ordering them in his mind. The doors opened, and Henry stepped on purposefully enough, got to his usual window seat in the corner and began to arrange his personal belongings as he had done for the last thirty years. Umbrella upright, between the kneecaps. Coat folded again and squashed in between him and the window. Briefcase slid under the seat, handle facing outwards for easy retrieval on arrival. Newspaper open on his lap. Satisfied that all his material possessions had been deployed correctly, he settled back for the twenty-minute journey to Pearse Station. Except that when he now looked outside, he saw that he was in Howth. He must have fallen asleep and had overshot his destination by five stations. Henry Gold prided himself on only a few things in his life, and right up there on the list was punctuality. In thirty years at the Natural History Museum, he had never once been late. Not once. Ever. His colleagues referred to him affectionately as Rain, Hail or Shine. 'Here comes RHS!' they would joke as they saw him make his way into the little office where the custodians would take their breaks during the day. Clockwork personified.

Henry reflected on the situation. The best estimate still meant he would be at least fifteen minutes late for work. He would have called, but he didn't have a mobile phone, despite Dawn's repeated attempts to what she called 'modernise him'. She said that he was turning into one of the fossils at the museum and that if he didn't watch out, they'd put *him* in a glass case too, and all the family would be able to come and visit him along with the other exhibits.

Nobody would have been able to explain, least of all Henry, why he did what he did next. He left his coat, briefcase and umbrella on the train. He got out and began to walk, down to Bull Island and along Dollymount Strand. Once on the beach, he took off his shoes and socks, and left them behind too. He continued barefoot, picking a path among the pebbles and odd scraggy shell. He felt the cool morning breeze in his hair, and looking up, admired the arching flight of a seagull overhead. He reflected that he was probably entitled to a day off after all his years of service. He told himself that when he saw a phone box, he would call the museum and then call Rose. A few minutes later, he remembered that he'd left his wallet in his coat pocket. And his coat on the train.

Cristelle's Diary

Make-Up
© Collins English Dictionary
make-up *n.* 1. cosmetics, such as powder, lipstick, etc., applied to the face to improve its appearance. 2. a. the cosmetics, false hair, etc., used by an actor to highlight

his features or adapt his manner of arrangement of the parts or qualities of someone or something. b. the art or result of applying such cosmetics. 3. the manner of arrangement of the parts or qualities of someone or something. 4. the arrangement of type matter and illustrations on a page or in a book. 5. mental or physical constitution. ~*vb.* make up. (*adv.*) 6. (*tr.*) to form or constitute: *these arguments make up the case for the defence.* 7. (*tr.*) to devise, construct, or compose, sometimes with the intent to deceive; *to make up a song; to make up an excuse.* 8. (*tr.*) to supply what is lacking or deficient in; complete: *these extra people will make up our total.* 9. (*tr.*) to put in order, arrange, or prepare: to make up a bed. 10. (intr.; foll. by for) to compensate or atone (for): *his kindness now makes up for his rudeness yesterday.* 11. to settle (differences) amicably (often in the phrase make it up). 12. to apply cosmetics to (the face) to enhance one's appearance or so as to alter the appearance for a theatrical role. 13. to assemble (type and illustrations) into (columns or pages). 14. (*tr.*) to surface (a road) with tarmac, concrete, etc. 15. (*tr.*) a. to set in order and balance (accounts). b. to draw up (accounting statements). 16. make up one's mind. to decide (about something or to do something): *he made up his mind to take vengeance.* 17. make up to. *Informal.* a. to make friendly overtures to. b. to flirt with.

Drop Dead Gorgeous

Drop Dead Gorgeous is a revolutionary new concept in make-up. The products aim to reflect your inner moods through colour. Cristelle Gold drew her inspiration for the range at a time of great personal upheaval. She was reading *Elle Décor* one day and came across the following piece of advice: *Make sure you express yourself with the right flowers for the right occasion*. It took Cristelle just a fraction of a second to make the vital connection. If this is true of flowers, she thought, it must be equally true of make-up. Make sure you express yourself with the right make-up for the right occasion. It was that simple! Drop Dead Gorgeous is more than a beauty product. It's a revolutionary new philosophy. The time had come, Cristelle reasoned, to see cosmetics in a new and glorious light, as representing something much greater and more noble than mere mechanical enhancement, concealment, artifice and trickery. Drop Dead Gorgeous make-up is for the modern-day Amazonian woman in you. It is about revelation, communication, self-expression. It is about courage. These women are sending messages. Let's take a look at what they are saying:

DROP DEAD GORGEOUS LIPS

DDG L001	Tulip Red	Declaration of love
DDG L002	Candytuft	Indifference
DDG L003	Carnation Deep Red	My broken heart
DDG L004	Chrysanthemum Red	Passion
DDG L005	Geranium Scarlet	Consolation
DDG L006	Golden Rod	Precaution
DDG L007	Honeysuckle	Devotion
DDG L008	Jasmine	Transport of joy
DDG L009	Jasmine Carolina	Separation
DDG L0010	Indian Jasmine	I attach myself to you
DDG L0011	Spanish Jasmine	Sensuality
DDG L0012	Jonquil	Affection returned
DDG L0013	Lotus Flower	Estranged love
DDG L0014	Lilac Purple	First love
DDG L0015	Orchid	Beauty
DDG L0016	Campanula	Constancy

DROP DEAD GORGEOUS BLUSHERS

DDG B001	Pansy	Thoughts
DDG B002	Damask Rose	Twilight
DDG B003	Poppy Red	Atonement
DDG B004	Lily Orange	Flame
DDG B005	Ranunculus	Truth
DDG B006	Rose	What's in a name
DDG B007	Burgundy	Beauty within
DDG B008	Deep Red	Passion
DDG B009	Full Red	Empowerment
DDG B0010	Geranium Rose	Preference
DDG B0011	Passion Flower	Faith
DDG B0012	Myrtle	True love

DROP DEAD GORGEOUS EYESHADOWS

DDG E001	Amaryllis	Pride, timidity
DDG E002	Anemone	Expectation
DDG E003	Arum	Ardour
DDG E004	Stephanotis	Exotic travel
DDG E005	Sunflower	Devotion
DDG E006	Chrysanthemum White	Truth
DDG E007	Columbine	Folly
DDG E008	Columbine Purple	Resolved to win

DDY 8009	Daffodil	Regard
DDY 80010	Daisy	Innocence
DDY 80011	Sweet Pea	Parting is such sweet sorrow
DDY 80012	Tuberose	Voluptuousness
DDY 80013	Verbena	Pray for me
DDY 80014	Violet Blue	Faithfulness
DDY 80015	Witch Hazel	A spell
DDY 80016	Rose Yellow	Pure joy
DDY 80017	Rose White	Truth
DDY 80018	Bluebell	Everlasting love
DDY 80019	Mimosa	Secret love
DDY 80020	Lily Yellow	Gaiety

Omega's Blues

Omega didn't get out of bed the next morning. On waking, he reflected that going to work just didn't feature among that day's list of effective possibilities. It was outside the range of do-able. He lay on his back, staring at the ceiling and wondering what was it, exactly, that might actually respond to the definition of do-able today. He concentrated on staring at the ceiling. Breathing. Expertly deflecting painful memories.

The next morning he didn't get out of bed either, a decision that was to some extent motivated by incumbent depression, and to a much greater extent by a massive full-frontal hangover.

By the third morning, he was beginning to part ways with reality. He was even deluded enough to think that nobody in work had noticed his absence. This, despite the fact that Adam had phoned him at least five times by now, leaving voice-recorded messages of varying length and description. The last one didn't even raise a smile: 'If you're not dead, phone me back.'

Omega was not dead. But he wasn't very alive either. He was beginning to feel the grim satisfaction of the pseudo manic-depressive who has finally understood the utter weirdness of normality; he even felt a certain tender-hearted largesse for Adam's banal and clumsy attempts to 'snap him out of it'. (The single worst approach to curing depression.)

By the fourth morning, Omega had given up all pretence of feigning illness, even to himself. He had gone beyond pulling a sickie. He had entered the lunar phase. The phase of nirvana-like calm. Beyond misery, beyond panic, beyond caring.

On day five, his boss rang him and said that he'd save him the trouble of coming up with some pathetic excuse for why he had jeopardised their most important project in the last decade and that he had one hour to haul his ass in to his desk, failing which he (his boss) would personally see to it that he (Omega) would never work in Dublin again. Omega reflected that while he may well be a manic-depressive, now was not the time to be a complete idiot.

Mr Fitzsimmons

Mr Fitzsimmons glared balefully at Omega over the top of his polished gold-rimmed glasses. *Armani*, thought Omega, who had been well trained by Cristelle. *All the better to stare at my employees with.* The soft morning light streamed through the window, glancing off the top of his bald pate and reminding Omega of a polished stone egg Cristelle had once bought in a market for its organic quality. Whatever about organic, its resemblance to the stone egg was uncanny. Omega reflected that he looked more like a poxy Buddha than ever today. He couldn't help redressing him in his mind's eye, draping a brightly coloured saffron or orange robe around his bony shoulders, replacing his shiny black leather loafers with a worn pair of brown leather sandals, rearranging his features a little so that the scowl he was wearing was more like a kind of serene trance-like gaze of deep contemplation. The high-powered walnut desk and Philippe Starck swivel chair would have to go. A cushion and a low-lying table would do nicely, a vase with a single white flower. Perfect.

'Omega?'

Omega started guiltily in his chair. He became uncomfortably aware that he had been staring back at his boss for the last five minutes, in total silence.

'Mr Fitzsimmons?' he rejoined.

The kindly Buddha threw him a look of utter disdain and began to toy with his silver-plated letter opener in a manner that Omega found vaguely threatening.

'Omega,' the Buddha pressed on, 'it is most likely unnecessary to remind you that you have not been in work for five days now, have made in that time no effort whatsoever to communicate your whereabouts, in fact have failed to respond to various and repeated attempts by Personnel to contact you, and have to date utterly failed to produce a single cogent reason to account for your absence.'

Personnel, in the person of Helen Carter, had left him a string of phone messages, and when that didn't work, had resorted to sending him text messages. She had started out polite enough: 'Helen Carter, Personnel here, just wondering where you are, Omega. Hope everything is okay. Do let us know when you get a chance.' Apart from that ominous-sounding 'us', Omega nearly responded to that one. Nearly, but not quite. Then the messages had become a little more intense, a little more Helen and less Personnel. 'Omega, um, I don't wish to be the harbinger of bad news, um, but you *really* need to contact us asap as, um, I can't cover your ass forever.' The last message was just Helen: 'Omega, you exasperating git, Fitzy is getting on *my* case about this too, so if you don't move your ass, I might be packing my boxes with you and need I remind you that you are *not* Jerry McGuire and I do *not* have a goldfish.' Mostly, the texts were more minimalist, for obvious technical reasons. The last one was like some kind of post-modern statement. It just said 'Omega :(?'

Sitting in Mr Fitzsimmons and Associates' wood-panelled sanctuary, Omega felt unaccountably cheerful. He had a sudden strong adolescent urge to respond to Mr Fitzsimmons with his favourite line from 'Comfortably Numb': 'Your lips move but I can't hear what you're saying.' But the urge passed. He mumbled something incoherent instead. In reality, he felt like a schoolboy who had been hauled into the headmaster's office for a good talking to. Like the time he and his friend had planted grass seed on the top of the Virgin Mary statue in school and she had sprouted a miraculous Mohican-style hairdo to the rest of the students' delight and the tight-lipped fury of the Christian Brothers. He hung his head in an apparent pose of remorse. He fidgeted in his chair. He felt, but couldn't see, the mute support from the other side of the closed office door. The normally noisy office had gone quiet when he had walked in. Adam had given him a thumb's up from behind his computer screen and mouthed 'good luck'. The others threw him sympathetic glances. Helen pulled a clown face and widened her eyes in a kind of I-tried-to-warn-you way. For a moment, he had felt almost jaunty. 'What's with the long faces?' he'd wanted to say. 'Pull it together.' As though he should be comforting them and not the other way around. He made scissors movements with his fingers, Omega-speak for 'cut it out, you guys', which half of the staff members got, and the rest put down to post-alcoholic binge shakes.

'Omega,' Mr Fitzsimmons was saying, 'I'm not sure I have your full attention.'

Oh but you do, thought Omega grimly. *Yes, SIR!*

'I'm listening,' he heard himself say in a strangely high-pitched voice. It came out as a squeak.

'Omega, I have to put this in your file. You understand that this kind of conduct is not acceptable. You have left me with no choice but to give you a final written warning. The next time you pull a stunt like this, you're out. Got it?'

Omega got it. He looked Mr Fitzsimmons straight in the eye. And said slowly, 'Now you listen to me, you poxy two-faced egg-pate lizard. You can take the final written warning and put it where the sun don't shine. I quit!'

What he actually said was, 'Yes, thank you Mr Fitzsimmons. Thank you, thank you.'

Omega hobbled out of the office and closed the door behind him. Once clear of the sanctuary, he bolted for the coffee machine, where he caught Adam and Helen in mid-conspiratorial huddle. They stopped talking as he approached, their faces two interrogation marks. 'Well?' said Adam. 'Well,' answered Omega, 'as of today, I am a dead man walking. Life without parole at Fitzsimmons and Associates. *Next time you pull a stunt like that, sonny boy,*' he said, perfectly imitating the Corkonian singsong accent of the Buddha, '*you're—*' The last part of the sentence was drowned out by a sudden coughing fit of Helen's. She was coughing so hard that Omega broke off the performance just in time to see Mr Fitzsimmons's spindly shadow precede him. 'So the opening went well,' boomed Adam in an unnaturally loud voice, beaming and nodding vigorously at Omega and Helen. 'Very well indeed.'

The Pontoise Experience

Cristelle emerged from the soft cream-scented world of Diptych, crossed over the road, turned right and disappeared into the red-brick municipal building that stood a little way down on the left. She smiled at the guy behind the tiled counter, who winked at her when he gave her the change, making her blush deeply. Ticket in hand, she hurried up to the first floor of uniform blue and white changing cabins overlooking the pool. It all seemed very efficient, very trim and neat. Each of the doors locked from the inside and featured identical centrally placed spy holes about the size of a two-euro coin. A lecture she once attended on Foucault's description of Bentham's Panopticon came to mind. *Discipline and punish*, she thought, *the swimmer-prisoners scurry to their identical cells in which they can be observed, without knowing it, through the oculus.* The various signs posted on the walls reinforced her initial impression of order and severity: '*Dèfense de faire ça! Shorts et bermudas interdits! Déchaussez vous–ici! Ne plongez pas dans le petit bain! Bonnet de bain obligatoire!*'

How we humans love our rules, Cristelle reflected, the more the better. She had barely made it past the first cabin when someone hollered, '*Chaussures!*' When this had no effect, there was a second, louder shout: '*VOUS LA BLONDE LÀ! VOS CHAUS-SURES!*' Glancing up, she spotted a bathing attendant on the opposite side of the third and final floor glaring down at her and pointing insistently at her shoes. Cristelle made a don't-arrest-me gesture and bent down to unzip the offending boots. Just then, her own floor attendant materialised and, taking her ticket, pointed huffily at the black line she'd just so nonchalantly crossed over, after which it was barefoot or flip-flops only. Cristelle gave the guy her wide-eyed I've-got-it look, which worked. He backed off, muttering something incomprehensible under his breath.

Ten minutes later, she was lowering herself into one of Paris's most fashionable swimming pools. Naturally it was Pierre who had told her about it. 'It's where they shot the film *Bleu*,' he'd informed her, ever eager to flash his cultural credentials. Cristelle had seen *Blue* and *White* and had always intended to rent *Red* on DVD, but had never got around to it. Not that she was about to admit that to Pierre. 'Oh yes,' she said, 'Juliette Binoche plays the grief-stricken musician's widow who looks and talks suspiciously like Juliette Binoche and who divides her time between a lot of things, including a swimming pool and a glass mobile, that are, well, blue. That's not counting the fact that's she pretty blue herself the whole way through.'

'That's the one,' Pierre admitted, giving her an odd look. He rarely got her sarcasm because his ego denied the possibility that someone might fail to take him as seriously as he took himself. But sometimes, as then, she was in a danger zone. So to make up or just on impulse she said, 'I really must go there.' And so here she was, with the only tiny glitch being that the picture of order and calm one had from the aerial perspective of the changing cabins turned out to be a perfect *trompe l'oeil*. In actual fact, the entire pool was a Dante-esque swirl of bodies and getting more hellish by the second. Inhaling deeply, Cristelle pushed off and broke into an energetic over-arm that she could only sustain halfway up the lane, after which she made the mistake of glancing behind her. She was rewarded by the terrifying sight of a small army of swimmers pummelling through the water at speed, spearheaded by some kind of immense sea-faring creature sporting black goggles and a Dali-style moustache. The creature was bidding to make an illegal inside pass, a fact that suddenly spurred Cristelle to Olympian speed. They ended up parallel to each other, but hell would have frozen over before she slowed down, with the result that her opponent narrowly avoided a head-on collision with oncoming traffic. For the next half an hour things proceeded pretty much in this fashion, with Cristelle powering down the pool like a particularly determined hare being chased by a pack of hounds barking and snapping at her heels. When on her twentieth lap she felt the creature's hirsute paw clamp down on her left foot and squeeze it, she squealed in genuine fright before wheeling round to glare viciously in his direction. The creature just laughed at her. Infuriated, she increased her pace until she was practically flying down the lane.

Then, as suddenly as it had begun, the insanity stopped. When, ten minutes later, she finally glanced behind her, there was nobody there. As if by some invisible signal, the pool had all but emptied. She lingered for a while longer, observing the intricate patterns the light made on the pool's floor and the slow motion rolling grace of a large woman swimming in front of her who looked just like an underwater Botero.

Rose's Dream Diary

I had the strangest dream. I was walking in a garden. Daytime. It looked like the kind of garden you might expect to see in an early Renaissance painting. It was perfection. The trees were like cut-out paper shapes on planes of green and umber. The colours were harmonious. They had a kind of faded quality. It was restful on the eyes. I felt very calm. I navigated this two-dimensional surface, turning corners. At a certain point I looked down and discovered I was holding two white roses, one in each outstretched hand. I examined them a little more closely and saw that they were different. Different petals. Different shapes. But both white and in full bloom. There were pearls of water on the petals. There were roots growing directly from the blooms. There were no stems. And I thought to myself, I must plant the roses. If I don't, they will die. But by then there was very little in the way of plants and foliage in the area. I was standing in front of a grey wall. It looked like it was made of concrete. It was very smooth and very high. I looked up and glimpsed the sky overhead. I looked down and saw paving stones. They met the wall. I started digging with a fork in the gaps between the tightly fitting stones. And I was elated to discover fresh earth, lots of it, underneath. There were even some worms and I thought, that's very good, lots of fertile ground. So I planted the roses. And the next thing the wall's surface was a mass of intertwining blooms. And I was left with this profound sense of relief and gratitude. Of love.

Thursday _ Untitled

Two roses in my hands
Each a frosty white
The petals curved like crescent moons
The loveliest of sights

117

Take these roses to the wall
Where the earth meets the sky
Plant them with your shaking hands
Lest they fade and die

When I grow old
I will recall
The lovely blossoms
By the wall

Salami

Pierre had decided to hold a seminar at the Eiffel Tower. He moved that day's class to 8 p.m. and told them all to meet him sharpish at the foot of the eastern pier. They had a special group booking and planned to ascend to the summit, with a brief stop on the way down to look at design elements in Jules Vernes. Cristelle was five minutes late, *comme d'habitude*, and could see Pierre tapping his Louis Vuittons impatiently as she approached. 'So kind of you to join us,' he said tetchily on her arrival. Unfazed, Cristelle murmured a general good evening and extracted a pen and notebook from her soft suede bag. From his expression it was clear they'd been waiting for her and he was irritated. He inhaled deeply and pinched the bridge of his nose with his thumb and forefinger, striking an attitude of profound thoughtfulness. The bunnies hushed up. Cristelle just managed to stifle a yawn. He looked, she mused, like a hen about to lay a golden egg.

'*Et la violà!*' Pierre announced into the silence, throwing out both arms in a kind of cosmic bear hug of the Champ de Mars and what had to be – the thought just then struck her – one of the biggest phallic symbols ever to have been erected by man. 'All 7,300 tonnes, 300 metres and 1,665 steps of it,' continued Pierre, 'built for the Centennial Exposition of 1889 by a bridge engineer, a certain—'

'Mr Eiffel,' Cristelle heard herself say.

'Thank you, Cristelle,' Pierre sneered, 'we are all amazed by your superior knowledge.'

The bunnies giggled a little nastily, but Cristelle was ready.

'Not bad for a stupid foreigner,' she shot back, smiling sweetly.

Pierre curled his upper lip at her and continued, 'As we go up, I want you to think about the iconic qualities of this masterpiece and to translate this into the world of make-up. Tomorrow I would like you to tour the souvenir shops in Paris and make a list of Eiffel products: note the packaging and the presentation, the colours, lines and concepts that this masterpiece has produced. Because *notez bien*,' he cautioned the assembly, 'this tower is much more than a mere architectural feat, it is a living and breathing monument to successful mass marketing.' Cristelle had to admit that here, finally, he had a point.

Ten minutes later, the giant yellow lift began its slow ascent into the guts of the wrought iron pillar. Cristelle found herself staring down at Paris like Gulliver must have stared at the rooftops of Lilliput. She felt gigantic and tiny at the same time. Pierre was talking to a select group of bunnies in the corner. She had somehow got separated from them by a wall of American tourists. Her deep reverie was interrupted by a conversation two girls were having in front of her. One of them was of the classic American blonde variety. The other was pale and on the anaemic side. *French*, thought Cristelle.

As though on cue, the American inquired, 'Where are you from?'

'Switzerland,' said the girl.

'Oh,' said the American. She had clearly assumed French too. 'So what do you speak there, French or German?'

'German,' said Miss Switzerland a little guiltily, like she was owning up to some hideous crime.

'Oh,' said Miss America. 'Is Switzerland closer to France or Germany?'

'Germany,' sniffed the Swiss girl.

It wasn't exactly *Mastermind*, but Cristelle had to admit she wouldn't have known the answer to that last question.

They fell silent for a minute or two, then the Swiss girl asked, 'Where is your hottle?'

The American drew a blank. 'I'm sorry,' she said, 'my what?'

'Your hottle,' said the Swiss girl, as if the other must be a bit deaf. 'Where is your hottle?'

The American looked embarrassed, then she was struck by sudden inspiration. 'Oh! You mean my *hotel*.' Nervous laughter. 'It's in the Latin Quarter.'

'Very nice,' said the Swiss girl, a little tightly, thought Cristelle.

'So have you been to see an opera or ballet since you've been here?' inquired Miss Switzerland. Cristelle pricked up her ears. *That* was a leading question if ever she'd heard one.

'Oh yes! I can't wait. I'm going to see *Salami* on Saturday,' Miss America said brightly.

Cristelle coughed to hide a snort.

'*Salami?*' asked the Swiss girl, looking blank in turn.

'Yes, *Salami*,' said Miss America. 'I can't wait! I booked it on the internet before I came.'

It was obvious the Swiss girl hadn't got it but didn't want to own up.

'I tried to get a ticket for a ballet,' said America, 'but it was booked out. What about you?'

'I saw a ballet,' Switzerland said, a little viciously.

Their conversation was suddenly killed by the lift attendant, who announced they had reached the top floor in ten different languages, something that took quite a while. The last thing Cristelle heard was Miss America on the way out: 'God, my feet hurt!', an exclamation which was met with silence from her new *freund*.

Miss Smiley

The girl in the recruitment office gave José-Maria a long appraising look, smiled briefly and nodded at him to follow her into the interview room. He did. When they were inside, she closed the door and invited him brightly to take a seat. Still all smiles. He sat. She took out his CV and put it on the table between them. His life, the abridged version. He had never seen the point in not elaborating on his past experiences. Not that he ever lied straight out. Just a tweaking here or there – assistant might become second-in-command, six months might become a year to fill in the odd gap or two, adequate became proficient and so on. A helping hand to self. Nothing more.

'So,' she said.

'So,' he parroted obligingly. He was hoping not to have to say anything too technical in English. He wasn't sure his linguistic skills were up to it.

'Have you been in Ireland long then?'

'For three days,' he answered, grinning back. He knew the Irish were famous for being friendly, but he was beginning to feel a tad uncomfortable with Miss Smiley here.

He reminded her of a younger version of Benicio del Toro. She flicked her hair a little self-consciously.

'And you have somewhere to stay?' she queried, the smile giving way to a look of almost maternal concern for his well-being.

'Oh yes,' he hastened to tell her. 'I am staying with friends – eh, my girlfriend.' The last part was more wishful thinking than anything given Dawn's reaction. As for 'staying with', that was also only true in a limited kind of way. Dawn's father, Henry, had sat him down on the night of his arrival and told him he was happy to let him stay for ten days in his home, until he found suitable accommodation, after which time, he'd be even happier to see him move out. Amazing what you could communicate if you really wanted to.

'Good, good,' the girl nodded, a little too quickly. The smile was fading.

Rats, Del Toro has a girlfriend, she sighed inwardly. *Just my luck.*

'So I see you've had various jobs, um, nightclubs, bars, gardener. Ah,' she said, 'here's an interesting one, salesman in a garage.'

'That's right,' he said. Well, nobody said a salesman had to necessarily sell cars, right? If she interpreted it badly, it was hardly his fault.

'Right,' she said. 'Well, let's send you round to Rent-a-Car for an interview. The pay's not very good,' she cautioned, 'but it's a great atmosphere, lots of young people work there of all nationalities and I know that they need someone for the Spanish team.'

If it's so great, thought José-Maria, *why aren't you working there yourself?*

But instead, he flashed her his best grin and said, 'Wonderfool, thank you.'

She didn't blink.

'I'll call you and let you know when the interview is.' They shook hands.

He resisted the temptation to wheel around at the doorframe and deliver his Arnold *hasta la vista* line (omitting the baby). It used to work quite well with foreign tourists when he was fourteen and they were completely drunk. However, given that in the present circumstances neither of these essential conditions were met, the outcome was unpredictable. So he just gave a little wave instead. Nothing over-friendly. But, he liked to think, kind of endearing at the same time.

When he left, it had just begun to rain, a soft drizzle in a lead grey sky. He made his way down the quays, as far as the Ha'penny Bridge. Then he changed his mind and doubled back, past the recruitment office, where he glimpsed Miss Smiley through the slatted beige blinds, grinning at some tall geeky guy who looked Irish. He kept walking as far as USIT, where he went in and peered at the accommodation notice board: *looking to share two rooms, non-smoker, cat lovers only* (unsuitable on two counts; not that he hated cats, just that he'd rather not live with one and be expected to love it); *girl only* (downright sexist); *looking for roommate and foreign language exchange* (definitely did *not* like the sound of that). By now he was beginning to feel hungry. Maybe it was time for a spot of lunch.

Dreamjobs

The tall Irish guy smiled back at the girl behind the desk.

'Omega,' he said for the second time.

She raised an eyebrow.

'I know, it's an unusual name. What can I say? My parents were into Greek Classics,' Omega said with a self-deprecating shrug.

The girl was still thinking about Del Toro and wondering if there was any way she could haul him back in for a second interview, but she made a sincere effort to pull herself together and get professional.

'Right, ha, ha,' she laughed obligingly. 'Well, so you are thinking of moving jobs then?'

'That's right.'

'May I ask why?'

For some reason, Omega felt completely unprepared for this question. It wasn't like he could tell it straight. *My boss is a moron, my wife is barely speaking to me and lives in another country, I'm depressed…*

'Just thought I could do with a new challenge,' he said lamely.

You look like you need a new challenge like a hole in the head, thought Sheila, a.k.a. Miss Smiley. *More like some Prozac and a couple of jump-leads.*

'A ha,' she nodded. 'A new challenge.' She cocked her head to one side, so that Omega felt he was being observed by some kind of homing pigeon.

'That's right,' he said, a little on the defensive side.

Ten minutes later they shook hands.

'We'll be in touch,' cooed Miss Smiley. 'So nice to meet you, Omega.'

The truth was that Omega was entertaining the fantasy where you go to your boss and tell them to stuff their job. Then you make a dramatic exit (amid your colleagues' standing ovation) and the next Monday start off at a brand new firm who pay you twice what you earned before and give you Franklin-style R-E-S-P-E-C-T. *Not going to happen*, drawled the little voice in his head. *Dream on, sonny boy!*

100% Moi

Cristelle lingered under the zebra striped awning of what in her guidebook was referred to as the 'million-aire's supermarket'. So basically, she thought, if it wasn't packaged in shocking pink, black or white, and didn't have a massive gold F stuck on it, it simply wasn't Fauchon. Pierre was inside, happily snapping up jellied fruits, a jar of rose petal preserve, several glass pots of foie gras and champagne mustard, all for a little dinner he was planning in honour of the bunnies. That, unfortunately, included herself. She could see him making his way around the pristine white interior, happiness incarnate, sniffing at the products on the shelves, twirling each one around in his hand and reading the labels as though a modern-day Moses had just descended from the shocking pink counter and handed him the definitive version from Mt Sinai. Thou shalt not cook thy duck without thy truffle mustard; thou shalt not kill the venison with nasty wine vinegar whenst thou can purchase Fauchon balsamic vinegar instead; thou shalt not covet our beautiful products – thou shalt get a life and buy them for yourself; remember the Sabbath day: we are open; thou shalt not murder, unless someone has eaten your *millefeuile à la vanille de Bourbon* without your permission; not forgetting, of course, honour your Fauchon and your Mother. Pierre was now standing impatiently behind a large group of Chinese tourists, who between them looked like they were carrying half the store home. Just then, Cristelle's gaze fell on a little sign in the shop window: 'Fauchon informs you,' it said rather stiffly, 'that the Restaurant is closed to be nicer, and will welcome you again in 2007.' She was still smiling at the rather suggestive translation when Pierre tapped her left shoulder, glowing with consumerist fulfilment. 'Shall we?' he asked, swinging his purchases like a male version of Holly Golightly.

'After you, Monsieur,' laughed Cristelle, warming to him unexpectedly. He may have his faults, she thought, but he was entirely and utterly himself.

The Octagon Bar

Dawn was holding a crisis council in the Octagon Bar. She had summoned Julie, Sarah and Jacintha the night after José-Maria's arrival and told them point blank that they had better show or else she would consider all bonds of friendship formally dissolved. She now peered at the confessional group over her gin lemon and wondered where to begin.

'So what's the big secret, Dawn?' snapped Julie rather irritably. This extraordinary council session had cost her an appointment with the hairdresser and a Sunday lie-in with Toby. Sarah shot Julie a venomous look and turned to Dawn.

'In your own time, Dawn,' she said breezily, reaching for a pistachio nut and expertly shelling it with immaculately manicured nails.

'So the door rings last night and I answer it,' Dawn began, scanning her micro-public to make sure she had their full attention. Everybody seemed to be concentrating, even Julie, who had stopped speed-texting Toby.

'And guess who it is?' Dawn proceeded, watching her friends' faces carefully for any sign of napping. But they were all being remarkably well behaved.

'Who?' they sang out in chorus.

Dawn opened her mouth to reply, relishing the moment of *dénouement*, anticipating the horrified expressions and cries of 'oh-my-god', but instead, Jacintha got there first.

'Oh my god!' she shrieked. 'You are *not* serious! He followed you from Spain!'

The others, including Dawn, now all turned to Jacintha, who sat back on her seat and threw her hands dramatically in the air. *You'd swear it was her crisis*, thought Dawn, feeling a little annoyed that she had been robbed of the moment of revelation.

But the heads soon swivelled back in her direction.

She didn't speak, merely nodded in grim confirmation.

Sarah looked suitably horrified.

Jacintha had frozen with her hands in the air. She was a bit like the statue of St Teresa in Ecstasy by Bernini in Rome, the one that looks like she might float off any moment and ascend into the sky like a giant helium balloon.

Julie whistled under her breath, then began to giggle. First it was subtle enough; Dawn thought she might just have gone into shock or something. But then she snorted out loud, spurting a jet of lemon vodka into the air, and turned a deep shade of puce. She was laughing and trying not to at the same time, and the result was highly disconcerting. Finally she gasped out, 'Oh god, sorry, Dawn, but I just got this flash of your expression when you opened the door! I couldn't help it. Sorry,' she concluded lamely, sobering up. Dawn looked injured, then she remembered what Jack had said. Soon they were all laughing. When they left, Julie said the extraordinary meeting had been absolutely worth missing her hair appointment for. Dawn decided to take the comment at face value.

Not that it resolved her problem, thought Dawn, but at least she felt a bit better.

Rose Lands in Charles de Gaulle

'Goodbye now,' said the air hostess in a slightly nasal voice as Rose walked past her to exit the plane, flashing her that nanosecond smile again. That 'now' was deeply irritating somehow. Rose felt like she'd just been patted on the head and handed a biscuit.

Once she had cleared the first corridor, she opened her handbag and fished out Cristelle's last letter. She stared at the address again, even though by now she could have recited it by heart. They were in the main arrivals area. Her fellow passengers milled around her in a blur of jackets, coats and hand luggage. The river of human traffic was being funnelled into a series of long glass tubes. She felt a bit like Augustus Gloop emerging from the chocolate river en route to the land of the Oompa-Loompas. She admitted to herself as she wandered along that Henry's reaction worried her. She was no Shirley Valentine, she reminded herself sternly. She was doing this for Omega and Cristelle. It had nothing to do with her marriage. She had decided to come and she hadn't told him because she knew he would have said she was meddling. That they needed to sort it out for themselves. That she had to stop trying to run their lives. So she had simply bypassed any possible objections and left him a little note on the kitchen table, under the butter dish. The note, she felt, was at least reassuring. 'Dear Henry,' it said in a most civilised tone, 'I have booked a short trip to Paris. I will be staying at the Golden Tulip Hotel in St Germain. I'll be back next Sunday. R.' She re-read it in her mind's eye and could find no fault with the contents. For a second, she actually entertained the idea that Henry would fail to notice her absence. He had been like Hamlet's ghost recently – more than living in the house, he seemed to be haunting it, moving around from room to room morosely in his soft padded slippers. Of course he would notice she had gone, she corrected herself. But would he care? She left that question unanswered and concentrated on locating the rest of her baggage instead.

Hi Dad

'Omega?'

'Hi, Dad, everything okay?' Omega was reluctantly making his way back to reality at Fitzsimmons and

Associates after his little time-out in Dreamjobs. His father sounded like he was far away. He could hear noise in the distance, now loud, now receding. *What was that noise?*

'Dad, where are you? Is that water in the background?'

'Um, yes, it's the sea. I'm at the seaside.'

Omega waited for a sequitur, but none seemed to be forthcoming.

'Right, of course,' he said, in the tone of voice of someone who should have known that. Then he braced himself and said, 'Dad, what are you doing at the seaside? Aren't you supposed to be at work?' The irony of the conversation wasn't entirely lost on Omega. His father didn't seem to have heard. There was silence on the other end of the line, then the familiar voice again.

'Omega, I've been trying to contact your mother to, um, let her know I've been a bit sidetracked. But there's no answer.'

At this point, Omega was beginning to get seriously concerned about both his parents' mental health. What was his father doing at the seaside on a Thursday afternoon? And why was he so worried about contacting his mother?

'Dad, you know Mum often goes to the shops and things. I'm sure she'll be back soon. What about you, when are you, eh, coming back?'

'Oh, I'll be home on the usual DART,' said his father.

Omega began to feel a little relieved. *Judge not and you shall not be judged*, he thought.

'Right then, that's fine. Um, if I hear from Mum, I'll tell her you called.' Omega knew it was highly unlikely he would hear from his mother. She had point blank refused to have anything to do with the whole mobile phone phenomenon, claiming darkly that it was sure to be the next biggest health scandal after cigarettes.

'Right oh,' said his father. 'Bye then.'

'Bye, Dad,' said Omega, trying to sound cheerful. 'See you later.' He pressed the silver button with the little red phone symbol and then decided to turn the damn thing off altogether. Sometimes he felt like his whole life was punctuated by a series of beeps and ring tones and smileys. I talk on my mobile phone, therefore I am.

It was *alienating*.

Cristelle and himself had made a pact when they were out together to turn them off. That was after one evening in the local Chinese restaurant where they had been sitting near a couple who spent the entire time talking into their phones instead of to each other. It was bizarre. They sat there, ostensibly out together, but in reality he was having a date with his Motorola and she with her Nokia. Mr Motorola was talking really loud, too. At one point, Cristelle actually looked over and hissed at him. He blabbed on, completely oblivious, until one of the Chinese waiters asked him politely to lower his voice. He looked at the waiter as if he were nuts and not the other way around, but at least he toned it down. Meanwhile, Miss Nokia was treating everyone to a one-sided monologue that consisted mainly of repeating the phrases 'I don't believe you', 'Go on', 'Wi-erd' and 'Kookie'. It was fascinating to watch in its own way; it was as if there were actually four people out to dinner instead of two. During the course of the conversations, every so often Mr Motorola would lunge across the table with his free hand and grab Miss Nokia's tiny wrist and give it a good squeeze. She would flash him a coquettish smile and then instantly change expression, eyebrows knitted, just in time to shriek 'he SO doesn't deserve you' into the little metal object. The next second she'd be back looking at Mr Motorola, raising her eyes to heaven, and sliding out of the hand clutch to make yawning gestures with her little hand.

La Vie en Rose

Rose paid the sullen taxi driver, who barely cracked a 'Merci Madame' and stood at the entrance to the Golden Tulip. Once or twice on the journey in from the airport she had made an attempt at conversation, but she quickly realised that she was dealing with an entirely different species to the Dublin cabbie where verbalising, whether you feel like it or not, is basically compulsory. Mostly she found the drivers at home irritating. She didn't *always* want to talk about the weather, was not *always* inclined to tell them where she was going, why and for how long, didn't *always* want to know the story of their lives, the particulars of their existence. But just then she would have welcomed some harmless banter to while away the time. She desperately needed to tell someone why she was here and what she was planning to do, as if telling the reasons to another human being would enlighten her at the same time. It was a kind of confessional urge or a need for expiation. But there was no nudging the driver into talk mode. She gave up when on her third attempt he openly scowled at her in the mirror.

She went in through the revolving doors. As she entered, a couple stepped out the opposite side. There was something familiar about the woman. Rose caught a glimpse of her profile as she passed, but then she was obscured by the glass, and the next second Rose was inside the hotel and the couple had disappeared. The man behind the reception desk smiled encouragingly at her, taking in at one glance the slightly battered suitcase and somewhat dishevelled Rose. Dishevelled, but a handsome woman nevertheless. At almost fifty years of age, Rose was still an attractive female, her grey hair scooped into a loose bun at the nape of her neck, her charcoal grey turtleneck sweater and matching trousers highlighting her green and amber-flecked eyes.

She cleared her throat nervously and said, '*Je m'appelle Rose Gold. J'ai réservé une chambre.*'

The man seemed to think that this made perfect sense, and nodded emphatically.

'*Oui, Madame, bienvenue à l'Hotel Tulip. Vous avez dans la chambre numéro 34. Voici les clés. On va vous porter les bagages tout de suite.*'

Shopping with Luc

Luc stood in front of the mirror and admired himself quite openly. More particularly, he admired the shop assistant standing behind Cristelle, who was also nodding in approval. Cristelle looked a bit distracted. When he asked her for her opinion, she just nodded and smiled. *She is physically here*, he thought, *but mentally she is a million miles away*. A bit put out, he focused on the shop assistant instead. In reality, Cristelle was panicking. She could have sworn she had just seen her mother-in-law get out of a taxi and walk into the Golden Tulip like it was the most natural thing in the world. In a 'I'll just pop into the Londis and get a few eggs' kind of way. *But it simply isn't possible*, Cristelle repeated to herself for the hundredth time. For one thing, Rose Gold had never flown anywhere in her entire life. She was terrified of flying. For another, Rose never travelled without Henry. Never. In all the years Cristelle had known her in-laws, their holiday patterns had been as predictable as the migratory flights of the swallows. A week in Kerry. A few days up North to visit relatives. A couple of weekend breaks 'beyond the pale', as Henry was fond of saying. That was it. Rose and Paris were just not made to co-exist in the same sentence. It was conceptually flawed, a semantic nonsense. And yet, Cristelle hesitated. Could she really have mistaken the familiar features and gait of Rose Gold? Or was it perhaps possible that she, Cristelle, was finally losing it? Or – and she had to concede it was within the realm of the possible – had the real Rose actually materialised at 5 Boulevard St Germain? Either way, it was a kind of insane scenario.

At the Hotel

Nobody would have agreed more with Cristelle on that last point than Rose herself, who by now had unpacked, showered, and tried – unsuccessfully – to phone Henry at the museum to forewarn him of her absence. She had got through to Albert, Henry's colleague, who had been at the museum nearly as long as Henry himself. He sounded a bit odd on the phone. 'Oh, hello, Rose,' he said. He seemed embarrassed or something. 'Looking for Henry, I suppose?' he enquired rather unnecessarily. He made a throat-clearing sound and said hesitantly, 'I rather thought you would know where he was.' A pause. Rose could feel Albert on the other end of the line, waiting for a hint. But she was quite unable to come to his rescue. She had heard Henry leave that morning. Clockwork Gold. She hadn't any reason to suppose that he was heading anywhere else.

'He didn't call in?' Rose was trying to sound calm, but her heart rate had suddenly soared. She could feel the blood pulsing in her temple. She felt a migraine looming. 'Not that we are aware of,' said Albert diplomatically. 'I'm sure it's just a little misunderstanding.

Nothing to worry about.' Rose was grateful that Albert was remaining characteristically calm.

'Right,' she said, at a loss as to what to say next. 'Eh, thanks, Albert. Talk to you soon. I'm sure he'll turn up any moment now.'

'Right oh, Rose,' said Albert. 'All the best now, you take care.'

Rose hung up, feeling a little defeated. As far as she was concerned, Henry's quotidian presence at the museum was one of life's few certainties and his unexpected absence was disconcerting, to say the least. Rose was the last person on earth who you would expect to take refuge in alcohol, but on this occasion, she thought she might just allow herself a small sherry, to steady her nerves.

She made her way down to the lobby and into the bar. There was a middle-aged man sitting in the corner, reading *Le Monde*. A young woman nearby was fussing over a small boy who had just expertly spilled the contents of his glass of fizzy orange on his shirt and the hotel carpet. Apart from them, the bar was mercifully quiet. No music, no television. Rose sank gratefully into a chair at a table by the window, and contemplated the street scene outside. She suddenly wished that Henry was there beside her so that they could chat about their observations. Not that you exactly 'chatted' with Henry these days, but before Hannah died, they had often indulged in a little commentary on the lives around them. After that, he seemed to lose all interest in passing conversation, the miscellaneous and often random details to be gleaned from a life passing by a window. Not that Rose was necessarily a big fan of trivia either, but she was addicted to observing others, and often tried to imagine what their lives were like by reading into their clothes, or puzzling over the items they picked out in the supermarket, second-guessing their innermost secrets from the outer trappings of their existence. She found other people genuinely fascinating. Henry would sometimes nudge her gently in the DART when he caught her staring openly at someone for more than a reasonable amount of time. But generally speaking, the person who was the object of Rose's active imagination was perfectly oblivious to her gaze. Advertising and television was making the world increasingly self-referential, Rose thought, increasingly inward-looking and in a sense, autistic. There was a general deadening of the senses, the body's natural reaction to visual and sonic overkill.

Rose had been studiously avoiding the subject of José-Maria and had been mostly successful up to this point. But now, looking out the window in the bar, she couldn't help thinking about it all again, and wondering what to make of it. He had actually seemed like a very nice boy. Dawn, of course, was furious. They had stood on the doorstep screaming at each other for fifteen minutes until Rose was unable to desist from intervening and told Dawn to either take their argument away from the earshot of the neighbours or bring him inside. Dawn had reluctantly capitulated and opened the door wider to indicate that he might enter before stalking ahead of him into the kitchen. Jack was enthralled by the new guest. He couldn't stop looking at him with an expression on his face that was little short of open adoration. José-Maria was wearing a bright orange T-shirt with a giant purple number 8 stitched onto the front and back, a pair of blue jeans and some vaguely lunar-looking silver sports shoes. He had short, jet black hair which fell in soft spikes framing his face and almost covering his equally black eyebrows, dark eyes and good bone structure. He was undoubtedly handsome, thought Rose. José-Maria shot her a grateful look as he put his bag down in the kitchen and smiled, revealing a perfect set of white teeth. Rose was sold. She considered teeth to be a genetic imperative.

Henry was less accommodating. He eyed José-Maria with the air of someone whose task it was to observe a mutant life form arrived from outer space. If he had made any sound, it probably would have come out as a low growl. Dawn was glaring openly at José-Maria, who, undeterred, looked down at

Jack, who was now jabbing a bubble gun straight at his chest and threatening to shoot. He raised his hands in a gesture of surrender and beamed. As far as Jack was concerned, they were friends for life. But he shot a stream of bubbles at him anyway, just to show him who was boss.

Irish Film Centre

Adam was sitting on his own in the corner of the IFC, checking out the very cute blonde girl who was sitting nearby. She looked foreign. *Swedish maybe*, he thought somewhat optimistically. In Adam's imagination, Sweden was a nation that gave room for hope. She was chatting animatedly to a shorter, stockier and considerably less good-looking friend. They were surrounded by the spoils of a shopping frenzy. The floor under their table was littered with fluorescent plastic bags. Adam knew it was terrible to be so superficial, but what was a guy supposed to do, ask the short dumpy one out because he felt sorry for her? Chances of that happening were frankly slim to none. Not while he was less than a metre away from Legs Eleven. The short one suddenly swivelled her head in his direction and caught him staring over. He blushed furiously into his beer and hastily looked away. Adam was something of a disaster around women. Omega said it was all a question of vibes. He gave them out all right, but they generally went wildly off target. Faulty wiring, Omega had diagnosed. He just needed a little black box to unscramble the signals. Right. Excuse me while I log on to hopelesscases.com. He pretended to study the French film festival program (*she might be French*) and considered ordering another beer. Omega was late again. Bloody typical. Not that he had the faintest intention of going to any of those movies. Adam's idea of entertainment barely stretched beyond late night television. And if he did venture into the cinema, he invariably went to see the latest American no-brainer. But the IFC had a nice bar and good potential for scoring, if only he could do something about those crossed wires of his.

Chocolate Frogs

Dawn stared moodily at the TV screen. It was raining outside. She was already in a bad mood on the way home in the DART. All the hilarity of the crisis summit had dissipated as fast as the pleasant after-effects of her gin lemon. The girls had gone back to their lives and she was still stuck with hers. To make matters worse, she had found this bizarre note from her mother on the kitchen table. Gone to Paris! It made Dawn want to snort. She had always suspected that her mother had it in her to take flight, *but not now*, she inwardly wailed. Not in the middle of the José-Maria debacle. She disconsolately ate another Pringle and glared at the tiny people scurrying around their allotted fifteen inches. She switched over to MTV and winced at the implausibly good-looking presenter lounging on a furry yellow banana-shaped couch. The girl was bubbling and chirping happily about the chart list like some kind of stuffed wind-up parakeet. The effervescent natural blonde type. Hair not dyed. Eyes really that shade of blue. Dawn pressed the mute button. It didn't make her feel better. Finally, she just turned the whole thing off.

Jack padded into the room and sat beside her. He was carrying his favourite Dr Seuss book and a packet of chocolate frogs.

'Hey there!' said Dawn. 'How was school? Got your homework done?'

Jack looked at her for a moment and announced solemnly, 'I do not like green eggs and ham.'

'Right,' said Dawn. 'Jack you are.'

Jack curled up beside her on the couch. 'Where's José-Maria?' he asked.

'Don't know.'

'Why?'

'Don't know the answer to that either.'

'Where's Grandad?'

'Don't know.'

'Where's Gran?'

'Paris.'

'Paris?'

'Yes, Jack. Paris. Only for a few days. Then she'll be back.'

'Will we be going to Paris too?' asked Jack.

'Not tonight.'

'Dawn?'

'Yes, Jack?'

'Will you read me *Sam I Am*?'

'Okay. Brush your teeth and get into your pyjamas and then I'll come upstairs and we'll read it together, okay? But only if you give me a chocolate frog.'

Jack obliged cheerfully.

Back at the IFC

'Okay,' said Adam. 'One for the road then?'

There was no reply.

Not surprising, really, given that Omega had still failed to show up. Adam said it for his own benefit, in his head. He had whittled away two hours between beers, trips to the bathroom, and increasingly long and obvious stares at his Swedish neighbour. He told himself that he needed a little Dutch courage. Wrong country but good concept. He planned on shimmying on over any minute now and blowing her away with sheer natural charm. The thought kept him going. It was a way of conjuring up a vicarious alternative life scenario starring some guy who bore a canny resemblance to himself and which greatly improved upon the reality of this other jerk sitting on his own in a bar. And he really did intend on going over. Right after the next beer. But first, another trip to the bathroom. He left his jacket on the back of the chair to indicate temporary absence, taking only his mobile phone and wallet. He made an unnecessary detour past the Swedish duo on his way and this time Legs Eleven actually looked back. And smiled! Adam floated past. Inside the bathroom he imagined what he would say on his return, a little comment maybe, or compliment, said with just the right amount of self-deprecating wit. He examined his reflection in the mirror.

When he came back, she had gone. It has to be said that Adam was one to look on the bright side. *So now*, he thought, *I've got a really good reason to have another beer.*

Palais de Tokyo

Pierre was holding a seminar in the Palais de Tokyo, one of Paris's many trendy art venues. The exhibition space was full of what Rose's mother would have rather euphemistically called 'individuals'. Meaning another species of humanity. The people were so *branché* it was hard to tell whether they were part of the exhibition or just regular *homo sapiens*. One of the installations came with a little leaflet to provide the slower members of the public with a clue as to what was going on. The exhibition itself consisted of a kind of open-plan wardrobe, with miscellaneous items of clothing hanging from a fine mesh of criss-crossed lines overhead. The leaflet had disdained to make any concessions to good grammar. 'hang it all' it said at the beginning. No capitals in sight. The next line was almost equally cabalistic: 'no sewing – just hanging.' *Right oh*, thought Cristelle, frowning in concentration. The leaflet steered its semantic course determinedly: 'as darkness and destruction have invaded the world the idea was to reconstruct the future with a little bit of love and a lot of hangers.'

Uh huh. Got the hangers, thought Cristelle. *Where's the love?* Undeterred, the leaflet continued: 'hang it all is a collection of concepts held together by a super thread, ready to do battle for good and evil to create clothes for the post modern superhero in all of us.' Cristelle was doubtful that she fit the bill, but hey, reading on: 'glimpse of the future, where b is for beauty, s is for strength and the spirit of positive reaction is the key.' *To what?* thought Cristelle, fighting exasperation, but the leaflet pressed on regardless. 'imagine the freedom and spaciousness of just hanging, free of any constraint, a revolutionary new technique – the result of a subverted experiment.' Cristelle experienced a brief acid flashback to the fittings for her wedding dress and had to admit that, here at least, the authors finally had a point. 'hang it all,' the leaflet concluded, 'peace, love and fight the power.'

Right, thought Cristelle. *Sure. Peace, love and fight the*— 'Pierre! Hi!'

Pierre was gazing in open admiration at a pink T-shirt hanging over Cristelle's head.

'Isn't it wonderful?' he enthused, waving vaguely at the gigantic washing line.

Not for the first time, Cristelle experienced some profound doubts about Pierre's sense of aesthetics.

'Um,' she said, trying to sound non-committal. 'Interesting,' she added lamely and basically untruthfully.

Pierre didn't notice. He was too busy salivating over a pair of deep blue trousers and matching jacket. He motioned briefly at Cristelle to follow him. She glanced swiftly at her watch before moving off. She had told Luc she would meet him later. He was bringing her on a surprise date. She felt strangely uncurious about the rendezvous. Kind of detached. Dawn would have said her chakra was a pukey shade of green today. Seriously off colour. Most of the other students had already arrived, a row of eager bunnies sitting on the mushroom-shaped stools that sprouted sporadically in this palace of cool. Suppressing a sigh, she sank into the chair furthest from the front, hoping to be able to slip in a few discreet breathing exercises en route through the wonderful world of Pierre.

But for once, he didn't seem inclined towards his favourite oratory style, the stream of consciousness or soliloquy. No. Today Pierre was Mr Throw-It-Out-There. Had the US mother company got to him somehow? Snuck in a training session when no one was looking? A weekend retreat for the Europeans to tell them how to talk turkey? Whatever it was, it was disconcerting. Pierre was on some kind of crazy interactive mission. He kept pointing abruptly at the now frightened bunnies in the front, who had spent almost an entire year banking on the fact that nothing was expected of them except their undiluted attention and admiration. Now that they didn't have Pierre's words to hang onto, they literally dropped off the precipice. Straight into verbal garbage. Pierre was getting impatient. His little cabbages were failing to live up to his expectations. Somebody had turned the lights on and there was nobody home. Cristelle couldn't help suppressing a grin as she slowly counted to ten backwards, exhaling on the even numbers. Closing her eyes on the odd. She had half-opened her eyes on eight when she suddenly realised that Pierre must have fired a question in her direction on seven. The entire class was looking at her expectantly. All the bunnies had swivelled round on their mushrooms. Pierre was looking like he had just swallowed an everlasting gobstopper.

'I'm sorry,' she smiled as sweetly as she could. 'Could you just repeat that question for me?' Trailing off into a tinny laugh.

'I asked,' Pierre replied, distinctly miffed, 'what you were thinking of doing for your business plan?' Only he didn't say business plan, it was more like *bizniss plin*. But this was no time for an inappropriate fit of the giggles. 'Drop Dead Gorgeous,' said Cristelle, pronouncing each word softly but clearly.

A hush descended over the assembly. Pierre took an involuntary step backwards, keeping his eyes fixed on Cristelle, who, to give her her due, didn't flinch. Finally he looked away, upwards, striking the pose of a man deep in thought. It was a key moment. Cristelle waited. The bunnies waited. Pierre waited. Then finally, a reaction. Laughter. A kind of hee-hawing chortle that turned into a full-throated rattle of mirth. The bunnies joined in a little nervously. Cristelle limited herself to a smile.

'Cristelle,' he finally gasped, wiping the tears from his eyes, 'nobody will *ever* buy a product called Drop Dead Gorgeous. I know the Irish are not famous for their *haute couture*, but really, how could you ever think...?' More laughter. This time the bunnies were a little more enthusiastic.

Later on, Cristelle would refer to this as her personal chariot-of-fire moment. Leaving judgment behind. She continued to smile until finally the laughter subsided. Pierre was looking at her with an expression of supreme condescension on his face. Then she spoke.

'Pierre,' she said, 'you are so full of shit it is mind-blowing. You have a lifetime of mediocrity ahead of you. You are the reason I will succeed.' That shut the damn bunnies up. 'And,' she added for good measure, gathering up her bags and jacket and rising from her seat, 'someday you'll be giving a seminar on me, you arrogant shit.'

Even afterwards, she would have edited that last sentence out. (So many other words in the dictionary, as her father always said.) Sometimes she did, depending on who she was talking to. She couldn't resist rewriting it just a little. Adding a majestic toss of her hair here, a jabbing motion with her finger. But mostly, she told it as it was. And it continued to satisfy her, years later.

She omitted the sudden uncontrollable tears. The desolation of a grey Paris evening and her broken dreams. And the unbidden suspicion that crept up on her. That he was right. She didn't have a clue. She was just another wannabe passing through. Trying to make it. Make-up's version of a waitress working night shifts in Hollywood and explaining to her customers that she's really an actress.

A Night at the Opera

Luc was waiting for her at the top of the steps leading up to the entrance. He looked very dapper in his new navy coat and maroon trousers they had bought on their earlier shopping spree. Cristelle suddenly felt a deep affection for this man who had taken her under his wing in Paris. She brightened as she approached him, not wanting him to see the state she was in. She had found the time to pop into the café opposite and freshen up. Whatever else, Cristelle was a believer in a fresh application of make-up to lift one's spirits. It had never failed her before, and it didn't this time either. A quick coat of smashed cherry red lipstick followed by a thin layer of gloss. Just a touch of moss green eyeshadow and the vaguest *soupçon* of burnt orange on her cheeks. A drop of Insolence, the new fragrance from Guerlain, and she was ready.

Luc was admiring the sight of her long boot-clad legs, slender waist and broad angular shoulders. He beheld her as he might have done the 'Mona Lisa'. It was a mix of deferential and sexual. He was engaged in a kind of homage to the fair sex, embodied in this instance in the person of Cristelle. If he had been a religious man, you might have expected him to produce a small woven mat, roll it out on the ground before him and pray to the east. Being an atheist, he limited himself to a more prosaic thought along the lines of 'life is wonderful'.

They had a box all to themselves. Cristelle sat with one arm dangling over the plush velvet armrest. Luc studied the programme. She stared up at the ceiling above in open admiration. Chagall's blues and yellows were stunningly audacious against the reds and golds of the opera house. His watery figures seemed to swirl above her in a crescendo of ever-closer circles. And all those illustrious names, too, written in uneven letters. It reminded her of a futurist manifesto. Bizet, Mozart... Not for the first time, Cristelle appreciated the ability of the French to juxtapose the modern and the antique. She had thought the same thing at the Louvre, standing in front of the glass pyramids. How daring they were. How unafraid. The people below were scurrying to their seats like ants in a factory. She could see the orchestra in their dug-out, chatting amicably, polishing their instruments with soft cloths, then quietening down in answer to some invisible cue, all eyes trained on the director's baton. The lights dimmed. Luc capitalised on the cover of darkness to slide his arm around the back of Cristelle's chair. It wasn't an unpleasant feeling.

The stage looked like a Degas painting come to life. The ballet dancers floated across the open space in a series of coded patterns that kept exploding and expanding, like lotus flowers on a blue pond.

Cristelle was unaware that she was holding her breath. Luc was fighting with his left hand, which kept wanting to explore Cristelle's back and neck. Finally the hand escaped and made a break for it, travelling rapidly up her spine and, in its eagerness to reach its destination, squeezing the back of her neck a little harder than intended. Cristelle let out a little yelp of surprise. She glanced rapidly at the errant hand's owner but his face was in shadow, unreadable. She let the hand stay where it was, on probation.

The Meeting at the Stairs

Rose got up from her seat as the last applause died away and smiled engagingly at the man next to her, who immediately got up and pressed himself against his seat to let her pass. He was less *charmant* after she accidentally trod on his foot. She stepped into the corridor and headed towards the foyer, thinking she would take a look around the upper levels of the building. There was a set of glass elevators outside that looked inviting, but she decided on a whim to take the stairs instead. It must have been around ten steps later that she saw Cristelle and Luc coming down towards her. At first she just thought, *Wow, that girl really looks like Cristelle!* But then she thought, *Rose, that girl is Cristelle.* She opened her mouth but no sound came out. Luc glanced at the woman who was staring at Cristelle and understood how she felt. She really did look stunning that evening. Cristelle was busy fishing out her mobile phone from her bag; she could have sworn she felt it vibrate just now. She didn't look up. All she felt in that moment was the soft reassurance of the palm of Luc's hand on the small of her back, and the oddest sensation that she was being observed.

It was all over in a matter of seconds. Rose thought later that she must have looked like Lot's wife, standing stock still on the stairs, incapable of speech. The thought that Cristelle might have met somebody else had simply never occurred to her. Not that she was utterly blind to Omega's shortcomings. Far from it. But somehow she had always believed that her son and Cristelle were a winning combination. Through thick and thin. That kind of thing. Now here was Cristelle in Paris with some French man guiding her down the stairs at the opera. Rose knew that out of loyalty to her son, she should have perhaps drawn attention to her presence on the stairs. But it had all happened so quickly. Of course, she could run after them, create a scene. But what good would it do? Cristelle, Rose suspected, had very good reason to be angry with Omega. And if that were the case, who was she, Rose, to interfere? But wasn't that why she had come to Paris?

She was interrupted by the sound of the bell, calling people to retake their seats. Feeling a little cowardly, she slunk into the main hall and back to her seat. And despite her best efforts to fret about Henry and Omega and Dawn and that usurper on the stairs and Jack and the Spaniard, she thoroughly enjoyed the second and third acts.

Back at the Hotel

Untitled

I was walking up the stairs,
You were there but unaware
In your company another
Not your husband or your brother

When I turned to you to say
How strange to meet in such a way
You brushed past me unbeknown
Distracted by your mobile phone

Shall I put it down to fate
Seeing you out on a date
Or was it but a dream of you
The girl who once I thought I knew

But who am I to cast you down
To sow the thorns that stud the crown
When all is said, you have the right
To be with someone else tonight

Rose was deeply dissatisfied with 'mobile phone' but a certain intellectual rigour prevented her from inventing something else. Besides, it did rhyme obligingly with 'unbeknown'. Anyway, she wasn't planning on making this particular poem available to the public domain. Not now or ever. In fact, she made a little paper ship of it à la Jack, and set it on the table in the bar before tipping the remains of her night cap into a very unsettled stomach and making her way to room 34.

The Insect Dream

Rose was in a tunnel. Its circumference was barely one inch wider than her own all round. She elbowed her way in, trying to ignore the black oozy slime that dripped down in giant globules from the ceiling. She detected a faint smell of moss or lichen, as though the pipe were located in an underwater cavern. Somewhere inside her, she knew she was having a bad dream. But there was no getting out of it. Not yet. She was aware of Dawn behind her, complaining, telling her off, saying that they should turn around and go back, that it wasn't too late, that she didn't have to keep going. But she did. She crammed her body forward into the blackness, trying hard not to think about what lay ahead. Then she saw one. A tiny black spider scuttled out of the gloom and scurried raggedly past her, its legs making a rapid rattling noise on the pipe's metallic surface, like distant rain. Then it was gone. Dawn screeched behind her. Rose pressed on. The next spider was bigger. You could tell by the increase in volume as it rattled past. More than a real spider, it seemed to Rose like the shadow of a spider that had fallen out of the blackness, like a silhouette cut-out. As it went past, its body gave off a faint iridescent gleam, the colour of spilt petrol.

Rose's throat went dry. She swallowed hard, once, then nudged forward again. The next spider was as big as a hand. It went past slowly, its blank eyes shone milky white in the gloom. It seemed to be unaware of their presence. Rose felt her elbows give way under her; her legs, suddenly heavy, refused to co-operate. Dawn was whimpering, pleading with her to stop in a barely audible whisper. 'It's okay, Dawn,' Rose said, 'we're nearly there.'

'It's okay, Dawn,' she repeated, more urgently. 'Dawn?' Rose sat bolt upright in her bed in room 34, her eyes snapping open. For a moment she couldn't remember where she was. She thought she was still inside the dream. 'Henry?' she said instinctively, her right arm patting the empty space beside her. 'Henry?' But as she said his name again, she was fully awake and in Paris.

Omega Contemplative

To the casual observer, Omega appeared to be utterly engrossed in the painting in front of him. He stood, his hands plunged deep into his pockets, his head tilting downwards, his broad feet planted foursquare on the wooden floor, shoes pointing characteristically inwards. Everything about him suggested deep, unbroken concentration. In reality, he was a million miles away. His eyes glazed over the serene Dutch interior, the calm poise of the female protagonist barely denting his consciousness. He took in, without actually seeing, the brightly coloured minutiae of an exquisitely detailed Persian rug, the dull sheen of the silver ink stand, the tactile quality of the feathery quill in the woman's hand, the soft white light that suffused the entire scene. The rug had been pushed back so that it cascaded down one side of the oak table, revealing the gnarly polished surface underneath. Omega's gaze finally hit the vanishing point, the lines of the painting all converging on a single detail in the very centre of the painting: a large drop-pearl earring fastened to the woman's ear with an elaborately knotted blue ribbon. He was drawn to it without knowing why. What was it? Then it came to him, unbidden. A memory of Cristelle in bed reading, her long blonde hair obscuring her down-turned face, her hands moving over the pages in that peculiar way of hers, like a blind woman reading Braille. The picture on the dust jacket was of a girl with a pearl earring, soft blues and yellows came to mind, a French-sounding author. Omega struggled to hold on to the picture of Cristelle that had formed as fast as it was now dissolving.

He became aware of someone sighing rather loudly in the vicinity of his left ear. He turned towards the sound and found himself staring at the woman next to him, who was glaring back with steely intensity. 'Not made of glass then?' Omega joked somewhat feebly, taking a sideways step away from her at the same time. The woman ignored him.

He sidled over to the next painting, stabbing the little button on his audio guide like a petulant kid who has just been caught with his hand in the cookie jar. He'd paid five euro for the damn thing but was getting heartily sick of the nasal, honeyed commentary, which was clearly intended for the pictorially deficient like himself.

Omega wasn't especially interested in art anyway. Cristelle always had to drag him to the various exhibitions around town. He would follow her around, pretending he'd never seen her before, pulling stupid faces and generally trying to distract her peevishly from the people she kept giving all her attention to in the paintings. She would swat his unwanted interruptions aside impatiently, shooting him exasperated looks or just plain staring through him. Once she'd been so convincing that a guard had come up to them and asked her, 'Is this man bothering you?'

Omega continued to stare miserably at the next painting.

The truth was, he had absolutely nothing better to do.

The woman in the painting continued to steadfastly ignore him.

Wilkommen nach Irland

José-Maria slid his pert behind onto the long wooden bench that skirted the wall of the dimly lit public establishment. He arranged his few possessions around him: the free *Event Guide* he had picked up at the cinema; his wallet; a couple of postcards he planned on sending when he figured out how to ask for a stamp without provoking laughter; the beanie hat Rose Gold had insisted he borrow (something he wouldn't be seen dead in anywhere else except in this mizzerable climate). He extracted his last twenty euro note from the wallet, a sorry-looking scrap of a thing but enough for a couple of pints at least. He spent a long time staring at the fans on the ceiling. They somehow reminded him of drawings he'd once seen of Leonardo's flying machines. Maybe he could rip one off and strap it onto his back. Fly home. He ordered a Guinness, thinking, *when in Rome...* He suppressed a grimace at the first bitter black gulp after the creamy foam. He was careful to remember the smiley face first, a habit he had picked up on seeing Dawn do it once when she'd insisted they drink her national brew in Spain. He plopped his index finger in twice for eyes and then traced a big curvaceous crescent-shaped smile underneath. The smile came out a bit crooked. Kind of spooky looking. He turned the pint around. Sad Guinness.

He took another sip and transferred his stare to outside. The Christmas lights were up already. A gigantic neon snowman loomed over the road, one spiky hand throwing snowballs, rings of white light bouncing up and down in nothingness. Its yellow hat led a precarious existence on his round head, flashing now right, now left, now right again. It made him feel queasy just looking at the thing. He withdrew his gaze. Opposite him, there was a girl reading in the half-light. Her left elbow rested flat on the table, her right curled under her chin like a sleepy cat. Then she swapped hands, and with her left underlined some words on the page. He studied the *Event Guide*. He tried to avoid thinking about what he was going to do next.

A Strange Encounter

Omega, seven pints later, was labouring under the illusion that he was becoming increasingly lucid. He thought he'd just pop into the Globe for a last pint. What he was really doing was creating the conditions for making a drunken phone call to Cristelle (who in all likelihood wouldn't answer anyhow) and leaving an entirely inappropriate message on her answer phone.

He stepped into the comfortable gloom and headed for the bar. 'A pint of Guinness, please,' he said, flashing his best dazzling smile at the pretty barmaid. (*Why not? He was an abandoned husband, after all.*) What he actually said was, 'A gint of pinness, slease.' It turned out to be close enough. A few sips later, he became uncomfortably aware that someone was staring at him from the window seat in the corner diagonally opposite him. Some swarthy-looking guy with jet black hair. Omega looked back belligerently, thinking, *What are you looking at, you eejit?* The stranger visibly flinched and looked away. Omega, satisfied, got down to the serious business of getting too drunk to dial. But not for long. The guy at the window seemed to be moving, heading in his direction. As he approached, Omega couldn't help noticing the purple beanie hat the guy was wearing. How oddly familiar it seemed.

Henry's Decision

Henry came home at eleven o'clock. He found Dawn in almost total darkness in the sitting room, staring at the television. It would have been perfectly normal except it was turned off.

'Hey, Dad,' she said.

'Hey, Dawn,' he answered. 'Everything okay? Jack asleep?'

'Uh huh.'

'Rose?'

Dawn swivelled round on the couch, accidentally knocking an empty tube of Pringles onto the floor.

'Didn't you know?' she said, looking at him with genuine curiosity.

'Know what?' he replied, nonplussed.

'Maybe you should go take a look in the kitchen,' Dawn said, watching her father carefully. 'She left a note.'

'A note?' he echoed, hesitating at the doorway.

'Yep,' said Dawn, almost cheerfully.

'Right,' he said. 'Where?'

'In the kitchen,' she said, turning back to the blank television screen.

He continued to hover at the doorway, as though waiting for more information, but none was forthcoming. He scratched his head, suddenly tired.

'José-Maria?' he finally said, trying to sound as neutral as was humanly possible.

'Dunno,' came Dawn's voice from the semi-darkness. 'Last seen at 10 a.m. this morning.'

The conversation seemed to have come to a natural conclusion.

Henry walked into the kitchen and examined the little note clamped under the butter dish on the table. For some reason, when he read it, he felt utterly calm. Almost unsurprised. *Rose has gone to Paris*, he thought. *Ah. That's why she didn't answer my calls earlier.*

He looked up and saw his daughter peering at him from the hall.

'Dad,' she said, 'is everything okay with you and Mum? I mean, is there something you want to tell me?'

Henry looked back, an expression of mild amusement of his face.

'Dawn,' he said slowly, 'there are moments – and believe me, there have been many over the years – when you realise why it is you have never stopped loving someone. Not ever. And this is one of them. I am going to join your mother in Paris. Do you want to come with me?'

Dawn looked at him, thinking, *Yes.* And then said, 'No.'

Last Orders

So the stranger came up to the bar and ordered a Guinness. But the whole time, he was staring at Omega, who was staring back. José-Maria, because of the uncanny resemblance Omega bore to the Irish girl he had fallen in love with in Spain, and Omega, because of the uncanny resemblance the hat bore to the cherished beanie hat of his childhood.

'Last orders, ladies and gentlemen!' shouted the barman. 'Place your last orders now!'

'Guinness, please,' said José-Maria and Omega, in perfect unison.

The barman lined up two pints on the counter. They stood shoulder to shoulder. Omega and José-Maria watched them in silence, waiting for the creamy white froth to settle.

Omega moved first, stretching out his right arm and pulling the pint to his lips, drinking a long greedy gulp. José-Maria followed suit.

Finally, Omega spoke. 'Nice hat,' he said.

'Thank you,' said José-Maria.

'Where did you buy it?' said Omega, trying to keep the paranoid strain out of his voice.

'I didn't – buy it,' said José-Maria, looking at Omega closely. 'It's not mine.'

'Oh,' said Omega, taking another deep gulp. 'So whose is it then?'

José-Maria considered his answer carefully. 'I believe,' he said, trying to find the right words, 'it is my brother's girlfriend's.'

Omega was momentarily confused. Then he had a flash of inspiration. 'Maybe,' he said, a little sententiously, 'you mean it is your girlfriend's brother's.'

The Last DART

Had long gone.

José-Maria and Omega sat finishing their pints as the barmen cleared away the debris around them. Chairs on tables, pint glasses stacked in impossibly high towers, crisp bags and other traces of a night out tipped into black plastic bags. Eventually they asked them to leave, again. They moved away reluctantly.

'So, as I was saying,' slurred Omega as he tripped over the step on the way out and nearly fell headlong into the oncoming traffic on Dame Street, 'she left me.' José-Maria made sympathetic noises and tried to focus on something, anything, in order to stay upright. 'She left me,' continued Omega, oblivious, 'to go to Paris and do this make-up course and try to forget me.' That 'forget me' proved too much. Next thing, he was blubbering, bent over on the side of the pavement. José-Maria was at a total loss. He looped his right arm over Omega's shoulder and sort of swung the other under him, so that the two of them ended up in a kind of unintentional bear hug. Now it was José-Maria who was close to tears.

'I'm in love with your sister,' he wailed. 'I don't know what to do.'

Allo?

'Allo? Cristelle? C'est Pierre. Tu es là? Réponds-moi! Je t'en prie. J'ai besoin de te parler. Cristelle! Réponds-moi…'

Cristelle slept soundly on her fold-down bed in her miniscule Parisian bed-sit. Somewhere in her dream, a phone seemed to be ringing in the distance, but she was too busy applying the finishing touches to her Drop Dead Gorgeous summer range to have time to answer. 'Not now,' she snapped briskly at the spectral secretary who nodded sheepishly and scurried back to the fax machine. 'And get me a double latté!' she shouted after him for good measure. In the dream she ran her index finger over the smooth surface of her chrome and glass desk, admiring the inlaid DDG signature glass mosaic in the centre. She sat surrounded by her fabulous products, each one a triumph of contemporary design and creativity. Her lipsticks were encased in jauntily coloured boxes made of a super-light plastic material. The blushers nestled snugly in soft silk cases that buttoned closed. Her Seeing Is Believing eye pencils were simply revolutionary. Just one touch of the white-tipped wand on an eyelid and chromatic science did the rest, automatically choosing the colour that would best complement the pupil's natural eye colour. Her Hand in Glove foundation range was an architectural master-piece, a seamless structural fit guaranteed to enhance any complexion. She studied her Nail that Colour nails with infinite satisfaction. The colours glowed and faded according to the intensity of the particles of light absorbed at any point in time, so that at night, what had earlier in the day been an unabashed crimson became a smoky twilight pink.

Her secretary came back with the latté. Except it wasn't her secretary any more, it was Omega. He stood over her with a peculiar expression on his face, almost seraphic. He radiated light and energy. He was wearing a DDG T-shirt. He set the latté down on the desk, taking infinite care not to spill any of it. Then he looked her directly in the eye and smiled, a broad, open smile, and turned away. She sat there, her mouth opening and shutting like the little *poissons rouges* she had seen in the museum the day before, trying to speak but unable to utter any sound. Her hand reached automatically for the Styrofoam cup and closed around it. Her nails, she saw to her astonish-ment, had exploded into a myriad of colours. It was like seeing dawn break over the bay of Howth. She brushed away a sudden tear from her cheek, almost angrily. And just as abruptly, woke up.

Dublin–Paris

Henry sat on the plane as though it were the 8:05 from Booterstown. Briefcase slid under the seat below him, handle facing outwards for easy retrieval on arrival. Newspaper open on his lap. Dawn had seen him off at the airport. She had insisted on coming with him, even offering to drive him there. It was the oddest reversal of roles. Neither of them spoke much on the way there. José-Maria sat in the backseat, staring out the window. He had arrived home at 4 a.m. with Omega, both of them in a piteous condition. Dawn hadn't spoken to him since. She was being magnificently cool. The ice queen personified. Try as he might to dislike him, Henry couldn't help feeling a little sorry for this guy crouching miserably in the back. He even made a feeble attempt to venture into the realms of conversation.

'Late night then, José-Maria?' he said into the front mirror.

'Yez,' came the muffled reply.

'So you met my son Omega?' Henry continued, inex-plicably eager to talk to this abject presence sitting immediately behind him.

Dawn shot Henry a look, part-quizzical, part-exasperated.

An old man was crossing the road, his small dog trotting after him.

She braked just in time. The old man glared at her and then at Henry. She ignored him, then revved the engine and shot forward, narrowly avoiding slamming into the car in front of her. Henry pretended not to notice. Instead, he concentrated on José-Maria, who was looking back inscrutably from behind his shades.

'Yez,' he said. 'Omega. He's very nice. I was wearing his beanie hat. That's how we met.'

It was a bit of a non-sequitur, but the explanation seemed perfectly reasonable to Henry, who found himself unaccountably warming to the oily Spaniard.

Dawn merely raised her eyes to heaven and made a strange sound at the back of her throat, half-sneeze, half-snort.

They drove on in silence.

Follow Me

Someone was holding Rose's hand and whispering to her in a soothing, melodic way, urging her along, telling her not to be afraid. She resisted at first but soon found herself yielding to the mysterious presence by her side. For some reason the stranger's words and manner filled her with a profound sense of trust and purpose. She let herself be coaxed along like a child. Perhaps she was a child in her dream. Now they lapsed into companionable silence and Rose found herself walking through lush green grass interspersed with tiny alpine flora. The prickly flowers glinted like shards of fallen stars in a surrealist painting of an inverted universe. Above her, the sky was a deep azure and the sun a brilliant ball of fiery orange. They began to climb, and as they did the landscape changed, becoming increasingly rocky and bare. Rose noticed that the air felt thinner and cooler than before. She could taste salt on her lips. She felt, but did not know, that they were approaching the sea. They climbed up and up for what seemed like hours until they could go no further. Everything went very quiet then, as though someone had reached into her dream and turned the volume down. The stranger appeared to be waiting patiently for Rose to decide what to do next. She knew – somehow there was no need to ask – that turning back was not an option.

They had reached the precipice.

Looking down, she saw the ocean rolled out below her like an unbroken pathway of lapis lazuli, leading nowhere. Here and there craggy rocks tore jagged holes in the water's brilliant surface. The waves broke against them, sending a fine spray of white foam arching into the air. She watched, as though hypnotised, the scene below.

Finally, her companion spoke.

'It's time, Rose.'

She closed her eyes. The stranger spoke again in a voice that was gentle but firm. 'Now, Rose.'

She felt the lightest possible pressure on the palm of her right hand.

'Ready?'

They jumped.

On the way down, she had time to observe an extraordinary amount of things. She mostly saw images of her children, but there were others, too, of people long dead and forgotten. There were even some of perfect strangers, one in particular of an old man wearing a tweed cap who tipped it at her as she fell and wished her luck. She had time to wonder, but in an entirely detached way, whether or not she would die. She reckoned she had even chances. Odds on to fall on the rocks, odds on not to. Her last exhilarating thought before she plunged feet first into the cool ocean's embrace was that it didn't really matter, seeing as it was only a question of when, not if. What she wanted most at that moment was to keep floating downwards like this forever. But her body began to pull against her, urging her up. She struggled against it, but the harder she tried, the less effect it seemed to have. If anything, she just sailed upwards more quickly. The next thing she knew, she had broken the water's surface with a whoosh and a yell of surprise. She looked around her, but her guide was nowhere in sight. She felt the air rush into her lungs with incredible force. The sun's rays shone warmly on her upturned face. It was only then that she knew it was good to be alive.

Can I 'Elp You?

'Can I 'elp you, sir?' the man at reception enquired of Henry, who was standing in the hotel lobby, looking around him somewhat wildly as though he expected Rose to emerge at any moment from behind the heavy brocade curtains or gilded Louis XIV console tables flanking the ornate marble fireplace.

The voice made Henry jump. He wheeled round and found himself staring at a huge bunch of white lilies in a deep grey enamel vase. A man was peering through the stems at him with benign interest, one eyebrow raised ever so slightly.

'I hope so,' said Henry into the lilies' foliage, relieved that he didn't have to speak French. Because he couldn't have, in any case. 'I'm looking for Rose Gold. I believe she's staying here.'

The man smiled and said, 'I'm afraid we can't give out that kind of information.'

'You can't confirm whether my wife is here or not?' asked Henry, incredulous.

'I'm afraid not,' said the man, beaming.

'She's expecting me,' said Henry untruthfully.

The man hesitated, then lifted the phone. 'One moment, sir,' he said.

He dialled Rose's room number and pressed the receiver to his ear, waiting, tapping his pen on the little stand-alone calendar beside the vase.

'Mrs Gold,' Henry heard him say. 'There's a...' he broke off, staring pointedly at Henry – 'Mr Gold,' mouthed Henry – 'a Mr Gold for you.' The other eyebrow shot up. Together they formed an almost unbroken arc.

'Which one?' the man echoed, looking closely at Mr Gold.

'Her husband,' supplied Henry, glaring back, beginning to feel irritated by this mediator between the upper and lower echelons of the Hotel Tulip who seemed to know more about his wife's whereabouts than he did.

'No, no, Madame,' the man said, 'I can't put him through. He's not on the phone. But I could send him up.'

The man's expression was totally unreadable. He replaced the receiver slowly, as though he had all the time in the world.

'Well?' said Henry, trying to suppress a rising note of impatience from creeping into his voice.

'Your wife shall be with you in a moment,' the receptionist said, indicating the plush red divan behind Henry and adding, 'please make yourself comfortable.'

Comfortable was exactly what Henry was not. He sat on one of the armchairs beside the divan so that he wouldn't have to look at the receptionist head on. From the corner of his eye, he could see him studying his nails fastidiously, clenching his fingers and releasing them as though they were an underwater amoebic life form. The movement was disconcerting. Henry shut his eyes briefly, trying to focus on what he would say to Rose instead. But absolutely nothing came to mind.

Window

Cristelle sat on the window ledge, her left arm hugging her knees, her right trailing languidly over the building's façade. By now Pierre was into his fifth message. The LED light on the answering machine blinked furiously and repeatedly, as if it was having trouble keeping up. *I never realised how incredibly repetitive he is*, she mused as he repeated for the umpteenth time how valuable a student she was, how she absolutely must come back to class, how *'terrible'* he felt about what had happened. She had been very upset. But now, as she sat there, she felt incredibly detached. Almost totally indifferent. Pierre whined on and on, half in English, half in French. She was even beginning to feel sorry for him and was considering putting him out of his misery and responding when the tape ran out of space and cut him off in mid-flow. Silence at last.

Five minutes later, the front door buzzer sounded. She uncurled her legs reluctantly and swung them back into the room, jumping down lightly onto the wooden floor and padding across the sitting-cum-bedroom to the front door.

'*Oui?*' she said warily into the intercom. Surely even the neurotically fit Pierre couldn't make it through two districts in five minutes.

'*C'est Luc. Je peux monter?*'

'Luc,' she said, feeling relieved and happy. 'Yes, come on up.' She buzzed to let him in and heard the distant sound of the door opening below.

Luc bounced enthusiastically up the stairs, taking them two at a time. Cristelle hurriedly threw on a pair of jeans and a T-shirt, scooping her hair back into a loose bun, and splashed some water over her face. No time for make-up. She exited the bathroom and opened the front door, nearly head butting Luc, whose upper body was practically at a right angle to his lower in his eagerness to be already inside. They pulled up short and ended up Eskimo kissing instead, then blushed simultaneously and giggled a little awkwardly. Cristelle suddenly imagined Dawn raising her eyes to heaven and making that funny snorting sound of hers, saying something along the lines of 'what is he, the road-runner?' and making ostentatious vomiting motions with one hand clamped over her stomach. The thought made her smile despite herself. Luc grinned back, ecstatic. He produced a small bunch of brightly coloured gerberas from behind his back, vivid pinks and yellows and oranges. It only reminded Cristelle more forcibly of Dawn. *I'm doing it again*, she thought glumly, *living in Paris and thinking in Dublin.* Two parallel tracks that would never, ever meet. Her face must have betrayed something of what she was feeling because Luc was looking at her solicitously.

'*Ça va?*' he said.

'*Oui, oui,*' Cristelle replied quickly. 'Would you like a coffee?'

'That would be su-pair!' he cried.

Cristelle reflected that all this *esprit de largesse* might become a little grating over time.

Sorry Twice

Dawn had gone to pick Jack up from school and had left José-Maria in charge of dinner. On her way out the door, she had said the first complete sentence of the day to him: 'Make dinner and phone Omega to

see if he wants to drop over. I'll be back in an hour.'
José-Maria mightn't have spoken great English, but
he recognised an order when he heard one.

Jack was waiting for her outside the school gates, his
green parka zipped all the way up to his chin, his
hood up although it wasn't raining. *Not a good sign*,
thought Dawn.

'Hey there,' she called, stepping off the pavement and
making her way across to him.

'Hold it!' shouted the lollipop lady just as Dawn heard
a car screech to a halt, practically inside her left ear.
The lady glared balefully at her.

'Sorry,' mumbled Dawn uncharacteristically. Jack had
disappeared further into his parka. All she could
make out were his eyes, wide and brimming with
tears.

'Hey you,' she said, crouching down to Jack's size.
'What's up?'

'We got out early,' Jack said haltingly. 'I've been here
for twenty minutes.'

'Oh god, Jack, I'm so sorry!' said Dawn. Twice sorry in one day was surely some kind of personal record. 'Listen, how about we pick up some comics on the way home? And a couple of packets of chocolate frogs?'

Jack brightened somewhat. At least she could see his nose now too. He put his hand in hers and tugged her to move. She had been mercifully forgiven.

Paella

Omega accepted the invitation to dinner gratefully. He hadn't been eating properly in weeks – in fact, since Cristelle had gone to Paris. His flat was littered with empty six-packs and TV dinner foil wrappings. Just looking at it made him sink further into self-pity.

He greeted José-Maria like a long-lost friend, clapping him on the back manfully. Two fellow-sufferers in love. The kitchen stank of fish. Omega began to feel a little less happy about the prospect of dinner.

'What's that you're cooking up?' he asked José-Maria as cheerfully as possible.

'Paella,' came the reply.

'And that yellow stuff?'

'Rice with *azafrán* – how do you call it?'

Omega blanked and then had a sudden flash of inspiration 'Saffron?' he ventured.

'Yez.'

Omega lit a cigarette and inhaled thoughtfully. 'So you dropped my father off at the airport today?' he said, addressing José-Maria's back.

'Yez.'

'How did he...' Omega fumbled for the right words. 'Seem?'

'Seem?' asked José-Maria.

'Yes, well, seem, appear. His mood, I mean?'

'Ah, well, he reminds me very much of you,' said José-Maria kind of cryptically. 'I thought my family was nuts,' he added, grinning at Omega, 'until I met yours! You guys are seriously *loco*.'

For some bizarre reason, Omega was immensely cheered by this comment.

'It's true!' he exclaimed. *'Tienes razón mi amigo!'* and surprised himself by laughing out loud.

The atmosphere of convivial bonhomie in the kitchen was irritating, so Dawn hung out with Jack instead, who was temporarily back to his chirpy self.

They sat companionably in the sitting room, watching cartoons and munching their way through an exquisite selection of curly-whirlys, flying saucers, jelly snakes and liquorice allsorts.

Sorry Thrice

Over dinner, Omega was making a sustained effort to maintain this fleeting sensation of happiness he had felt earlier on. *The truth is*, he thought staring morosely at the dead fish in their shallow yellow grave, *I should have gone to Paris long ago and tried to sort things out with Cristelle.*

'Why didn't I go to Paris?' he asked the baby squid.

'Coz you ain't no good,' said the squid promptly, shooting him a venomous jet of black ink. Omega set his fork down beside his half-empty plate and sighed.

'You look like shit, Omega.' For a second he thought the squid was still speaking, but it was Dawn, surveying him from across the table.

'Sometimes,' she continued, ignoring José-Maria, who was kicking her under the table in an attempt to ward off whatever killing blow she was going to deliver next, 'you have to fight for things. You know? Go and sort it out. Go see about the girl. All that stuff.' José-Maria was nonplussed. *Wasn't that what he was doing himself?* But at least they agreed on something, he and Dawn. He withdrew his silver runner.

'She still loves you,' Dawn went on. Omega stared at her, open-mouthed.

'How do you know that?' he asked, a desperate glimmer of hope expanding in his chest like a helium balloon.

'Because she told me on the phone,' Dawn replied evenly.

'You've been talking to Cristelle all this time and never said anything?' Omega shouted, his hand unconsciously moving to the fork and gripping it in a totally threatening manner.

'Put the fork down, Omega,' Dawn said simply. 'I am her sister-in-law and I am her friend. If she had wanted you to know we were talking, I'm sure she would have said so.' Omega wrestled with the fork, which seemed to have taken on a life of its own, finally allowing José-Maria to gently lower his right arm to the table. Jack had been quiet all this time. Now he looked at Dawn and said defiantly, 'She was Mommy's best friend. It's her birthday today.'

Dawn and Omega were horror-struck. He was right. And they had completely forgotten. There was nothing to say. Jack was starting to blubber. Soon they all would be. José-Maria couldn't have explained why he did what he did next. He got up and went over to the sideboard, prised a stubby white candle loose from its ceramic holder and jammed it into the cheesecake Rose had left them. As birthday cakes went, it wasn't much, but the lit candle looked pretty in the darkening kitchen and the pale yellow cake glowed warmly underneath. He did all this quickly, with his back turned to the Golds. Then he flipped off the kitchen switch and, turning around, began to sing 'Happy Birthday' in Spanish. He didn't know how to say it in English. Mercifully, Omega and Dawn got the message and joined in, their voices clearly strained with emotion. But anyone who looked at Jack could tell it was an inspired move. He was the happiest he had been all afternoon.

Some time after 10:30 p.m., Dawn put Jack to bed. She rolled up the covers to his chin, the way he liked it, and switched on the bedside lamp. She smoothed his hair back, feeling sudden profound love for this little person. She ached for Hannah to be there. She would have known what to do. Fighting back tears, she whispered, 'Hey there, monster, how about a bedtime story?' Jack looked back and smiled. 'No thanks,' he said, in what sounded like a very grown-up voice. 'I need to sleep now.'

'Of course,' Dawn agreed quickly, trying to hide her disappointment. She would have done anything to make him feel better. She berated herself for having picked him up late from school. She hadn't known it would close early, but god, somehow she should have.

'Dawn?' said Jack.

'Yes, Jack?'

'I'm sorry about José-Maria's letters.'

That was too much. She wiped away a tear almost angrily from her cheek and, swooping down on Jack, hugged him for all she was worth.

When she could finally speak she just said, 'Actually, Jack, they looked pretty good in the end. Much better than the original version. Some day, you and me, we'll go to St Stephen's Green and set them free.'

'I'd like that,' Jack mumbled sleepily.

'I love you,' she whispered, then tiptoed out of the room and down the stairs.

Washing Up

Dawn found José-Maria at the sink, washing up. He looked kind of funny with those yellow rubber gloves on his hands. She took a tea towel from the cupboard, and without speaking, stood beside him, drying and stowing the plates as he washed.

'Omega?' she finally asked.

'Gone to Paris,' he said neutrally.

'Oh,' she said.

'Maybe I shouldn't have said anything, but he found the note and made me tell him where Henry was staying. I offered to go with him to the airport but he said he'd get a taxi.'

'Right,' said Dawn, although what she was actually thinking was, *My whole family is falling to pieces.*

'Thank you,' she whispered. 'For the cake, you know.' She said it so quietly that José-Maria wasn't sure he hadn't imagined it. He was vigorously scraping off the charred remains of marine life from a glass dish. He just shrugged his shoulders.

'I mean it,' said Dawn, turning to him now so that he had no choice but to stop what he was doing and look back. 'We've never dealt properly with Hannah's death,' she said quickly, before he or anyone else could stop her, the words tumbling out. 'We've always pretended it never affected anything and in reality it has totally screwed us up. It's like—' her voice broke, she was crying in earnest now, 'we just can't deal with all that emotion. It's too much. So we act like it never happened. All of us. We're such stinking cowards about the whole thing. Jack is the only one who is brave enough to want to remember.'

Her whole body was convulsing. José-Maria wrapped the rubber gloves around her and just held her.

The Night Shift

Omega was going to Paris. But just before he did, he let himself into Fitzsimmons and Associates and, waving cheerfully to the unsuspecting night cleaners, turned on his computer and proceeded to clean everything he had worked on for five years off the hard disk. 'Are you sure you want to delete this?' the computer kept asking nervously. 'Absolutely,' said Omega, hitting the enter button with grim satisfaction. Next he went into his mailbox and emptied that out too, releasing its contents into the ether like ashes scattered from an urn. It was a very liberating sensation. There was the internet to take care of, too, all those telltale tags in 'history'. He dealt with that quickly and then turned his attention to his little plastic models arranged neatly on the open shelves to the left. What to do? He studied the tiny plastic trees and houses and parking facilities, the suspended traffic lights that had taken him an entire morning to get right. He reached down and picked up a car between his thumb and forefinger, examining it as though seeing it for the first time. It really was exquisitely designed. Its miniscule glass windows glinted as he twirled it round. Its grooved rubber wheels spun obligingly on their axes. The white leather interior was radiant. The rainbow metallic finish was inspired. On impulse, he put it in his pocket. *It was never going to get more perfect than that.* Then he cleared away the trees, snapping their spindly trunks in one clean movement. The houses were a little harder; he levered them off the white board with his pen knife. Next came the traffic lights, the tram tracks, the level crossing, the pedestrians. 'You too, I'm afraid,' he told the elderly man walking his dog. He piled them all into one of his desk drawers and, making his way into Mr Fitzsimmons's office, opened the window and poured the miniature urban life out onto the street below. The cleaners had long since gone. Half an hour later, he let himself out.

Running Late

Would passenger Gold, Omega, travelling to Paris, please make his way immediately to gate five. This is the final call for passenger Gold, Omega. Your flight has now boarded and is awaiting immediate departure.

Omega pounded down the corridor, shot past duty free, and virtually dived into the outstretched arms of the girl at gate five.

'Passport, please,' she said, smiling, her palms raised like a warden halting oncoming traffic.

Omega backed up and handed it over, his heart thumping painfully in his rib cage.

'Boarding card?' she said, still smiling.

For a truly horrible moment he thought he'd left it at security. The guard had made him go back and empty out his pockets into one of those shallow plastic trays after the metal detector beeped at the tiny car.

'I think you'll find it's in your shirt pocket,' said the girl, pointing at his chest.

Omega fished it out gratefully and gave it to her. She tore off part of it and handed the other half back to him, then inserted her part into some kind of machine that chewed it up for a while before spitting it back out.

The plane puttered amicably down the runway. *This thing is never going to get off the ground*, thought Omega, but just as he did, it suddenly picked up speed, crouching low and purposefully at ground level like a skier about to launch into the void. Then it was in the air, wheeling in a great arc out over the rapidly fading contours of Dublin city and powering its way towards the open sea.

Omega's Last Word

Dublin, autumn 2006

Dear Mr Fitzsimmons,

Throughout the five years I have spent in your employ, nine out of ten of my projects were approved by various clients, not least of which most recently the Irish government. In that time, I have worked hard and consistently on all of these commissions, and have had occasion to be highly satisfied with the results of my endeavours. Over the past months I grant that my performance has slipped, something I regret, and that my attendance record has left much to be desired. As for your record over the same period, my dear Mr Fitzsimmons, I am afraid to say that I find it sadly inadequate. Your crabby refusal on several occasions to grant me annual leave has been a source of constant irritation, not to mention practical difficulty, in my life. Your insistence that you be given equal credit for my projects has always struck me as ungenerous and, frankly, misleading. Your inability to find any words whatsoever of praise or encouragement for work well done, coupled with your 'like it or lump it' attitude, has been consistently counterproductive to your own objectives. Your stubborn refusal to consider any pay rise over and above the rate of inflation has left me in poorer economic circumstances than those in which I took up my employment.

Yes indeed, I quit.

Omega

P.S. Were you to seek legal recourse in view of certain documents pertaining to my time here that no longer exist, I would caution you to ponder this line of action carefully, especially with respect to Project 11 and the highly dubious manner in which it was awarded. Trust me, I would have no hesitation whatsoever in producing those few e-mails and letters that I retained and which are now in my unfettered possession. I look forward to receiving my last pay cheque and other accrued benefits, savings scheme reimbursement, etc.

P.P.S. The fact that you are having an affair with Helen Carter of Personnel is none of mine or anybody else's business. I'm sure you'd like it to remain that way.

Why Are You Here?

The doors of the elevator opened and five Roses were standing there, the real one and the four reflected ones in the mirrored interior. The real one stepped out and the other four instantly followed suit, merging into the familiar form he loved so well.

'Why are you here, Henry?' she asked him, not unkindly. She seemed genuinely curious.

He had got to his feet the minute he saw her and was standing on the other side of a wicker coffee table, feeling a powerful sense of *déjà vu*.

It came back to him in a flash. They'd had an argument years ago, well before they got married, and she had broken off the engagement. He couldn't remember why they had argued, but he recalled standing in her living room and her father calling her to come downstairs, glowering at this young man who had anything to do with upsetting his daughter. And she had appeared, not out of an elevator, but around the corner, and framed in the doorway had asked him the same simple question:

'Why are you here?'

'It's always the same reason,' he told her now. 'Because I love you.'

The receptionist had a strange coughing attack and busied himself ostentatiously with rearranging the lilies.

'Things have changed, Henry,' Rose said. 'I'm not sure that answer is good enough.'

'I...' Henry stopped, collecting himself. 'We've already lost someone we loved. Please don't tell me I've lost you too.'

'It would have been her twenty-seventh birthday today,' whispered Rose. 'It never stops hurting.'

'I know,' said Henry. 'I know.'

Rose walked around the wicker table and straight past him towards the revolving doors. She was half-way there when she glanced back over her shoulder. Henry was standing looking at her, unable to move. 'Let's go, Henry,' she said firmly. 'You must be starving.' He opened his mouth to speak. No words came out. But this was no time to wait for her to change her mind. He caught up with her at the door and squeezed into the revolving triangle. They emerged simultaneously into the still Parisian night air. They walked past the front of the hotel, arm in arm, for all the world like a perfectly ordinary couple, still happy, still in love. And in a way, they were.

The receptionist sighed and discreetly checked the register. Yes, there was a double room still free, if Monsieur and Madame requested it.

En Plein Air

They sat outside the brasserie, to the left of the entrance, in the shade.

Cristelle ordered a Perrier and a *croque-madame*.

Luc ordered the *plat du jour*, which turned out to be a steak and *salade verte*, and a *demi bouteille de vin rouge*.

The waiter flapped around in penguin mode, his arms doing a thousand things at once. He reminded Cristelle of Mr Tickle, but she didn't attempt to explain why to Luc. Instead, observing Luc's monochromatic assortment of lettuce leaves cowering before the approaching fork, she said, 'Wow! When they say green salad here, they mean it!'

He shrugged in response, as if to say *'bah, alors?'*

'I mean, live a little!' Cristelle couldn't stop herself from adding. 'Would it be truly sacrilegious to put a tomato on there?'

'You must be the first person I've ever met,' Luc bristled, 'brave enough to criticise French cuisine.'

Her comment had genuinely irritated him. She was amazed. 'I'm just teasing, Luc,' she said. 'You know I love everything French.'

'Perhaps you would rather go to an Irish pub and eat cheese and onion crisps,' he sneered uncharacteristically.

She was stung by the remark but didn't let it show. It had been a stupid thing to say about the salad in the first place.

The next moment, several things happened at once.

She reached over to squeeze Luc's forearm in a gesture of reconciliation and ended up knocking the bottle of wine onto his cream linen trousers instead. He leapt up from his seat, as if he had been electrocuted, only to feel a stinging blow land squarely on his right cheek. For a wild second, he thought Cristelle had just slapped him with the force of a hurricane. But before he could speak, another punch had been delivered straight into his chest, winding him severely. He doubled over and dimly heard Cristelle shouting, 'Stop it, Omega! Omega!'

The next thing Luc remembered was waking up and seeing a little circle of people staring at him from what appeared to be an immense distance. The faces were peering down from above like the cherubim of a stuccoed ceiling. He instinctively put a hand to his face, but all his features seemed to be in their usual place. He must have blacked out. He could make out Cristelle clearly, her golden hair glowing in the sunlight, her face a study in maternal concern. Just behind her was a gangly-looking guy with dark hair and a savage glint in his eye. His assailant! The guy's right arm emerged from on high and Luc recoiled, but it was only to help him up.

Omega, PI

It was one thing imagining Cristelle in Paris. And quite another seeing her there. With someone else. Nothing had prepared Omega for how that would feel. He reflected, as he slunk along behind her and Luc, that part of the problem was that he had been avoiding feeling anything in particular for months now. Cristelle emerged first from the flat. Omega was waiting across the road, trying to be as inconspicuous as possible. He needn't have worried. She didn't even glance in his direction. He was on his feet immediately, and then almost just as quickly sitting down again, fighting off a sudden severe pain in his chest. The man who emerged after Cristelle looked, well, French. Omega wasn't a particularly good judge of physical appearance, and was inevitably surprised to learn from Cristelle that so and so was considered as being 'devastatingly cute' or 'drop dead gorgeous'. He wasn't self-conscious about his own looks, and by corollary was basically blind to everyone else's.

But right now, possibly for the first time ever, he was acutely aware of the existence of another male. They hesitated, as if debating which direction to go in, then veered left and left again, disappearing down a long flight of stone steps. Omega watched them, then panicked and started to follow. He hadn't intended to. His feet made the decision for him.

As he walked, he kept thinking that at any second Cristelle would glance back over her shoulder, tossing her hair in that familiar rapid movement he knew so well. Their eyes would meet. Time would stand still. The next moment she would be running back up the steps, collapsing into his open arms. At some point in this scenario she would murmur, 'Take me home.'

Reality Bites

'Tou total moron, Omega!'

'I'm sorry. I didn't think, I—'

'Just go.'

'I don't want to.'

'Leave!'

'No.'

'Leave me alone, now!'

'No.'

'Go, get, shoo – out of my life!'

'No.'

'It's over, Omega. I'm too tired. I can't think about this any more.'

'Cristelle, I made a terrible mistake. I wasn't *balanced*, for Christ's sake! I was angry with everyone and everything and nothing seemed to matter any more...nothing made sense...after Hannah, everything...'

'Don't you dare suggest this has anything to do with Hannah's death. Don't you dare do that, Omega.'

'I'm not. I didn't. I know it hasn't. But—'

'Don't!' Cristelle screamed with such vehemence that Omega took a step backwards, stunned by the sheer force of her fury.

Then she was in his arms all right, but only to take better aim. She pounded him with her fists, kicking and hitting him for all she was worth.

And in between punches she was shouting at him, 'So you've got the monopoly on pain, you selfish bastard? You thought you were the only one missing her? You are so full of shit, Omega! You, you, you! Always about you! Well congratulations, you insulated yourself from pain and inflicted it on me instead! Don't you get it?' she finally spat at him, all her strength gone. She was gripping his shirt. One of his buttons hung loose, attached by a single thread.

She was slipping to the ground, exhausted. Omega caught her before she could fall. She sat with her hair over her face. When she spoke, her words were barely audible.

'I'll tell you who Hannah was,' she said. 'She was my best friend. She was your and Dawn's sister. She was the only eldest daughter Henry and Rose will ever have. She was Jack's mother. She was all of these things, Omega. But that doesn't even begin to describe her. And all we can think about is who she was *to us*: our relationship, our grief, our loss. Don't you get it? It was Hannah herself who got the raw deal. She was the one who lost her life. And she's never going to have it back. Ever.'

Omega sat there, blinking. He felt a dull ache in his chest unlike any he had ever experienced.

In the end, it was Cristelle who broke the silence.

'Now,' she said, 'leave me alone.'

E-Mail to Dawn from Henry

Dear Dawn,

Your mother and I have decided to stay on for a while in Paris. We both feel we need to work some things out – for all our sake. Your Uncle Patrick has offered to look after Jack for you for the time we are away. Please do take him up on his kind offer. Jack loves being there and gets on very well with all his cousins. You have our hotel details, don't hesitate to get in touch if you need to. Your mother and I have discussed your desire not to return to school and we have decided to give you our moral and financial support. Please reply with a detailed career plan and salary expectations.

Life's too short, Dawn, as we all know, to be frittered away in pursuits that do not interest us. Please think carefully about your life and what you'd like to do with it. We are all ears.

We both feel, your mother and I, that the shock of your sister's death led you to grow up somewhat more rapidly than we might have wished. However, this may just be your natural character. In any event, to paraphrase the great James A. Michener, the time has come to follow your dreams and know them for what they are. Your mother – who is here beside me – has asked that I add that this includes José-Maria as well. Do consider, however (the thought just occurs to me now), that there is an excellent selection of apartments to rent that comes out every day in the *Evening Herald*.

All our love,

Dad and Mum

Dawn

Dawn re-read the mail for the tenth time, blinking rapidly. Then she texted Jacintha: *Lost it completely. Parents gone AWOL in Paris. Am I the only sane person alive? D.*

Jacintha texted back: *Let's hope not, for the sake of humanity xox J.*

The Musée d'Orsay

Cristelle was in the Café des Hauteurs on level five of the Musée d'Orsay. The woman who had been behind her in the long serpentine queue that morning was sitting on her own at the next table. Extracting a pocket mirror from her bag, she examined her reflection critically. She caught Cristelle staring over and half-glared, half-pouted in her direction. Cristelle rapidly gazed into the depths of her cappuccino. The gigantic glass and steel clock face shone impassively in the autumnal light. From where she was sitting, she could see the Sacre Coeur at eleven o'clock, and underneath it, in a series of horizontal stripes, Paris's familiar beige and grey buildings, a line of trees, a road, the quay and the Seine. Just then a boat made its way across the lower half of this strange time-bound canvas. Even though it was still early, the café was already bustling with tourists, streaming towards the pale green wicker chairs and calm wooden interior of the eatery. Cristelle's gaze was repeatedly drawn to the tiny Sacre Coeur looming spectrally in the distance. She held up her right thumb and it disappeared. She gave it the thumbs down, and it returned to view. She did this for a while, then sighed deeply, paid the bill and left.

'Doesn't it look strange, Henry?' said Rose, staring up from the café at Place Louise Michel.

'In what way, dear?' Henry enquired.

'Well, it's so dream-like, so ethereal. Don't you think it looks sort of fake? Like there's some evil genie in the sky ready to hoist the whole thing back up at a moment's notice.'

Henry smiled. 'Maybe it's been beamed in from another planet,' he said, 'and the real thing is somewhere else entirely.'

'Quite,' laughed Rose. 'You know, Henry, it says here that the Sacre Coeur is the second-highest point in Paris after the Eiffel Tower. You must be able to see it from practically anywhere.'

Dear Yellow Buddha

Cristelle sat at her glass-top table in her tiny bed-sit and contemplated the canary yellow ceramic Buddha she had purchased on a whim in Le Monde Aux Couleurs. The Buddha had somehow distinguished itself from the mass of candles, incense burners, beady purses and statuettes crowding the shop window. Every day since then, when she passed by the shop she'd been ridiculously happy to see no new yellow Buddha had taken its place. In front of the cross-legged mystic, she'd positioned an iris-scented Diptych candle she'd purchased on her way to the pool. A little to the right was the Japanese mobile her friend, Mina Ohta, had given her. Mina was Cristelle's only female friend in Paris. Her gaze now shifted to the three diminutive geishas tip-toeing after one another in eternal circles. Mina had explained that the geishas in question were actually *maiko* (geisha apprentices) and were wearing *yukata*, cotton summer kimonos with cherry blossom, butterfly and Japanese maple leaf patterns. The younger the geisha, Mina told her, the more colourful the *yukata*. Their jet black hair was in the *taka shimada* style, a high chignon habitually worn by young, single women. Each of the three had the traditional wide sashes fastened in the back with a large flat bow, called *obis*. Their hair was made from black thread and their outfits from folded paper. In her mind Cristelle referred to them as Maiko I, Maiko II and Maiko III. Each carried a large fan, one pink, one yellow and one green. In front of the mobile stood a tiny framed passport-sized photo of Cristelle and Hannah, when they were sixteen, and beside it a single orchid in a small glass vase. Looking at the photo now, Cristelle had a sudden insight that the group of objects she'd collected so thoughtlessly formed an altar of sorts, an impression that was reinforced by the long tapering shadows the candle threw on the Buddha's serene countenance. *Dear yellow Buddha*, she thought, *please tell me what to do now.* But the Buddha's eyes were closed and his lips were sealed.

Le Jardin des Plantes

'*Cedrus Libanotica*,' Henry read out to Rose. 'Brought from England by Bernard de Jussieu in 1734. Given to Jussieu by Collinson, an English doctor.'

'Just imagine, Henry,' said Rose, gazing up from the wooden bench circling the girth of the ancient tree, 'the stories it must have heard.' Henry patted the gnarled trunk absentmindedly, as though it were a beloved child.

'Isn't it amazing?' he said happily. They sat in companionable silence under the immense leafy pavilion of the oldest cedar of Lebanon in France.

'It's odd,' continued Rose. 'Maybe it should make me sad, but actually it makes me happy to think this tree was here over two hundred years before we were born, and for who knows how many after us. Don't you think it puts everything in perspective?'

'You know,' smiled Henry, 'I was thinking the same thing. Life persists, life struggles to continue, life prevails. At least that's what I want life to do.'

'Which is why it seemed so wrong,' said Rose, as though finishing an earlier conversation. 'It was too soon, Henry. Nobody was ready.'

'No,' Henry agreed, taking Rose's hand and turning to her. 'Least of all Hannah herself.'

'You think I'm being selfish,' she said, obscurely annoyed.

'No,' Henry said. 'It's not that. I think we all need to accept that she's gone. To let her go.'

'I'm trying,' said Rose in a tiny voice. 'But it's bloody hard.'

'All right,' Henry said in a strangely lucid way. 'Let's say we keep her here, every second, every hour, every day, until she becomes unrecognisable from the person she was. Would that be the best way to honour her memory?'

'Don't belittle me,' Rose said. She felt incredibly angry all of a sudden.

'For God's sake,' said Henry, 'I'm not belittling you. You know that's the last thing I'd ever do. Let her go, Rose. It's time.'

Omega's Plan of Action

'Leave me alone,' said Omega.

'Jeez, man, I just wanted to see how you were doing!'

'Not you, you idiot, that was what Cristelle told me three days ago. There's no way she's going to take me back. I saw it in her eyes.'

'Right,' said Adam. 'So what are you going to do now?'

'You know what?' said Omega. 'I have absolutely no idea. Jump into the Seine. Throw myself in front of an oncoming Métro. Unless you've got any better suggestions.'

'How about impaling yourself on the pyramid?' said Adam. 'Or something a little less spectacular, like trying harder?'

'Now why did I think you were going to say something just like that?'

'Like what?'

'Like what you just said – try harder! God, you sound like Fitzsimmons.'

'I'm pretending I didn't hear that. Look, Omega, you vacillated for three months before you got on a plane, and you think just showing up is going to cut it?'

'Not really,' Omega admitted.

'So you know what you have to do.'

'Come up with a plan of action?' asked Omega.

'Well, that's one way of putting it,' said Adam. 'Even a plan by itself would be a start.'

'But I can't face rejection!'

'Listen, mate, and don't take this the wrong way, but from where I'm sitting, you really can't afford to be that precious. And if I have to be completely frank with you, you already have faced rejection. That would be the part where she says "leave me alone".'

'Thanks for the reality check.'

'Move, Omega. Reflect, then act.'

'This isn't tae kwon do.'

'And it isn't semantics either. Listen, I'm spending a euro a minute here to tell you things you already know. So why am I doing that?'

'Because my misery somehow cheers you up?'

'Don't flatter yourself. Okay, I've gotta go. Fitzy has entered the building. POA, Omega. I mean it. Reflect—'

'Then act, I've got it. Adam?'

'What?'

'Why do you care?'

'Oh, shut up! Or I swear I won't.'

'You're a true friend,' said Omega, feeling alarmingly weepy.

'Yes I am, and you're a bona fide idiot if you don't fight for this. You two were made for each other. You know that. I know that. I'm betting even Cristelle knows that, somewhere deep down in her Gucci boots. But you're going to have to find a way of reminding her. Gotta go, Omega. Don't mess this up.'

'Bye,' Omega croaked, putting the phone back in his jeans pocket and ignoring the strange buzzing sound in his head.

Into the Woods

The taxi made its way almost noiselessly through the streets of Paris. Luc tried to put his arm around Cristelle, but she shrugged him off. 'I can't,' she said. 'I'm sorry. It never occurred to me he'd just show up like that.' Luc unconsciously rubbed his lower chest. The doctors had said it was only bruising, but it hurt nonetheless. What hurt more, though, was the thought he might lose her. Cristelle stared out of the window without really looking at anything. A soft rain drummed on the car roof, making all the street lamps seem hazy and out of focus. 'Night-time in Paris,' she said to no one in particular. 'The city of lights.' Luc looked at his hands.

Fifteen minutes later they were making their way through the Bois de Boulogne. The trees towered ominously overhead, like vast shadowy sentinels intent on blocking their path. The driver made some coarse joke about the nocturnal activities in the woods behind. Cristelle had a sudden vivid flashback to one time she and Hannah were being driven in a taxi through Phoenix Park. Their driver had made a comment along similar lines. They couldn't have been much more than sixteen at the time. Hannah had glared at him and said, 'Just drive,' jolting the smirk off his face in a heartbeat. *Where the hell are you?* Cristelle thought. *I could really do with talking to you now.* But there was never any response. Only the moment you were in and the profoundly depressing thought that you couldn't share it any more, not with that person, not ever again.

Omega Accidentally Has Coffee at the Cafe des Fleurs

Aimless as a cloud, Omega wandered down Boulevard Saint-Germain. He spotted a pretty café with a glassed-in veranda and thought he'd take a break: from doing practically nothing. Still, a break was nonetheless required. Anyone who feels sorry for themselves for three days, he thought, knows how exhausting a process it can be. But now the time had come to act. Adam's phone call had inspired a new sense of vigour and purpose in him and he felt he should capitalise on the positive energy immediately, or rather, after a quick sit-down. '*Un café crème s'il vous plaît*,' he told the waiter airily. Really, he couldn't account for it, he almost felt – what? Happy? Omega maintained his buoyant good humour until the *crème* arrived on a much-scrubbed silver tray, bearing a white china saucer and cup, two paper-wrapped sugar cubes, a spoon, a brown earthenware pot and a smaller white jug. He poured some of the delicious-smelling liquid into the cup, added some milk and sugar and stirred thoughtfully. As he did so, he glanced surreptitiously at his neighbours: an older, well-dressed man in deep conversation with an elegantly coiffed woman; a couple of Japanese tourists huddled closely over their cups and giggling behind their hands; a middle-aged couple, possibly American, looking proprietarily at the menu. The only other person on their own was some beady-eyed Frenchman reading *Le Figaro* and flapping the pages irritatingly close to Omega's right ear. Oh, and some woman in the corner, with enormously sad eyes. Just looking at her brought Omega back to earth with a thud. *What am I doing here?* he thought desperately. As though in response, the waiter flashed past his table and in one swift movement slid the receipt halfway under his tray. *I'm paying*, thought Omega, and the idea did not feel insignificant.

Time Warp

The taxi swung into a tree-lined avenue, its tyres crunching over the gravel so lightly it might have been soft snow, and pulled up at a turn-of-the-century pavilion strung with lights. 'Oh Luc, it's beautiful!' exclaimed Cristelle, meaning it. A porter materialised out of the shadows and, hurrying round to her side of the taxi, opened the door. She stepped out, wrapping her fine cashmere pashmina tighter around her shoulders. The restaurant was a myriad of glass gilt mirrors and plush Napoleon III furniture. Huge candy-striped drapes in soft creams and pinks hung from a semi-circle of sparkling windows in the *belle époque* interior, lit by crystal chandeliers and the warm glow of candlelight on generously spaced and immaculately set tables. The chairs were upholstered in a deep cherry red, matching the carpet. There was a flurry of activity when Luc and Cristelle entered the dining room, with several waiters appearing at once: one to take Cristelle's scarf, the second to seat her, the third proffering a menu. A fourth supplied her with a small footstool covered in rich velvet, for the comfort of her bag. A fifth was coming towards them pushing a chariot of fine champagnes. Cristelle chose a Deutz Rosé and Luc a glass of Pommery Cuvée Louise.

'So, what are we celebrating?' she asked, regretting the remark as soon as she'd made it. She had meant to sound amusing or blithe, but it came out as neither.

Luc looked at her a little wryly over the rim of his flute and said, 'Let's drink to a thing we call *espoir*.'

'Oh, we have that in Ireland too,' Cristelle said breezily. 'Hope is practically our middle name. At least, it used to be. Now it's expect.' She frowned involuntarily. Another thing she didn't want to do: criticise Ireland to the French, criticise France to the Irish. Luc laughed out loud though and cocked one eyebrow as he took a sip of his champagne.

'Shall I order for us both?' he asked.

'Oh yes, please do,' said Cristelle, 'anything except *escargots*.' He laughed again and with a practiced flick of his wrist summoned the waiter.

They started with the *amuse-bouches*, delicate little palate ticklers that arrived in a triumphant marine procession, each one more heavenly than the next. A melody of crab claws, salmon with coral cream, langoustines, poached quail eggs with black truffles and a circle of glistening pink tuna in philo pastry. Cristelle drained her flute and Luc ordered a bottle of Pouilly Fumé. The waiter complimented him on his choice.

'I bet they say that to everyone,' Cristelle teased him.

'Or maybe,' said Luc, 'just maybe, they meant it.' Cristelle looked abashed and started toying with the knives and forks on the spotless linen tablecloth. She couldn't understand what was wrong with her: where all this toxicity was coming from.

'Luc,' she said, looking across the oceanic expanse of white between them, 'I'm sorry. I can't relax. It's all...' she gestured vaguely around her. 'Too much. It's...' Luc reached across the table and put his right hand over hers.

'Shh,' he said, 'you're fine. You look radiant tonight.' His eyes were ever so slightly bloodshot, whether through lack of sleep or because this wasn't his first drink of the evening, Cristelle couldn't tell.

'Excuse me for a moment,' she told him, smiling palely.

As soon as she got into the cubicle, she bolted the door and, pulling down the toilet lid, sat gazing into space. She counted slowly to ten, exhaling on even numbers. *What?* she shouted inwardly. *What is it?*

'You're doing it again,' someone said calmly in the next cubicle. Cristelle snapped out of her trance and gazed around her. 'That thing you do,' the voice continued.

Cristelle didn't move. She waited.

'Hello? Are you still there?' the voice said.

Cristelle scrambled down to floor level and squinted under the door. There was nobody out there, yet she could have sworn there were only two cubicles.

'You can block me out all you like,' the voice continued, sounding a bit miffed. 'But I'll always be there, there's nothing you can do about it.'

Cristelle was electrified by a wave of panic and recognition.

'Hannah?' she gasped.

'Congratulations!' said the voice. 'I've been trying to talk to you for four years and you've finally deigned to listen.'

'Hannah?' Cristelle screamed out loud, flinging open the door and pushing wildly at the other cabin, which opened suddenly to reveal a spectacularly bejewelled madame who stared at Cristelle as though she were nuts.

'Woops!' said the voice, giggling.

Cristelle apologised to the woman and, wheeling round to the marble-topped sink, opened the gold faucet and let the water gush out at full speed. The woman couldn't wait to get out of there. She bolted past, shooting Cristelle a look to let her know she absolutely didn't approve of blonde foreigners clearly on drugs lowering the tone of the place.

'Hannah?' asked Cristelle urgently. 'Where are you?'

'More to the point,' came the voice, 'where the hell are you? Is this you, Cristelle? Is this who you are?'

'It's who I am right now,' said Cristelle defensively. 'And what the hell do you mean by "that thing I do"?'

But no answer came. Silence enveloped the room again, only now it had a denser and more solid quality than before. Cristelle stood at the sink, staring at her own reflection. Rose had once asked her casually if she'd ever 'chatted' with Hannah since her death. Cristelle remembered feeling appalled by the question and genuinely concerned for Rose's mental health. 'No,' she'd told her, and added without thinking, 'of course not.' Rose looked a little sad at that but had just smiled at her. 'Well, I do sometimes,' she'd said with a conspiratorial wink. 'But don't tell anyone I told you.'

Cristelle hurried downstairs and exchanged a few words with the maître d' on her way to the dining room. Luc glanced up as she arrived. 'Back already?' Cristelle did a double take. She was convinced that she must have been gone for at least twenty minutes. She slid into her seat and took a sip of wine, then spread her linen napkin on her knees and speared a sliver of braised duck. Five minutes later one of the waiters coughed discreetly behind her. 'Luc, I'm sorry, I think I need to use the bathroom again.' Luc opened his mouth to speak but she was already out of her seat and making her way to the foyer. Out of sight of the dining room, she quickly signed the Visa receipt at reception and thrust a twenty euro note into the head waiter's hand. He nodded briefly to show he'd understood. He held out her pashmina and led the way to the exit, shooing the porter out of the vicinity and opening the door for her himself. '*Bonne chance, Madame,*' he said, bowing solemnly as she was swallowed up into the night.

Must be an Angel

Omega was lying face up on the hotel bed, squinting through the round viewfinder in the white plastic light-box he had purchased earlier for Jack in the Louvre souvenir shop. He pulled back the little trigger on the side of the box with his right index finger and Giuseppe Arcimboldo's allegorical painting of spring snapped into view. He pulled it again: a shot of the Marly Courtyard; again: the statue of Psyche reanimated by the kiss of Love; again, Michelangelo's 'Dying Slave'; again, da Vinci 'Mona Lisa'. The pictures were projected onto a black background with the author and title written in small white capitals underneath. He pulled the trigger faster and faster and the images danced before his eyes, the half-armed Venus de Milo, the headless Samothrace, the

'Wedding at Caana', 'Liberty Leading the People'...
He was so engrossed in this miniature whirlwind tour
that he didn't hear the phone on the first ring. He
picked it up on the second. 'Monsieur,' he heard, 'there
is a call for you on line two.' Omega thanked the
receptionist and heard the line click.

'Hi, Dad,' he said in the most cheerful possible tone
of voice he could muster.

'It's your wife, Omega,' Cristelle said dryly.

Omega dropped the viewfinder. 'Where are you?'

'I'm on my way to your hotel in a taxi. Get dressed.
We've going out.'

'Right,' Omega almost shouted into the phone. 'I'll
get dressed immediately. I'll—' But the line went
dead. She'd already hung up.

Once she had got into the taxi, she leaned back into
the leather seat and shut her eyes, realising that she
had absolutely no idea about what to do next. All she
knew was that she had to leave. Now. The next
instant, her mobile phone vibrated in her bag. Praying
it wasn't Luc, she took it out and looked at the screen:

private number. She hesitated, debating whether to risk answering or not. Generally she never took calls from persons unknown – on principle. But. She studied it a moment longer then flipped it open. '*Oui?*' she said warily into the receiver.

'Oh hello, Cristelle. It's Henry here.'

Henry? Given what had happened back in the bathroom, Cristelle suddenly felt really frightened.

'Henry in person?' she asked quickly.

'Henry in Paris,' he replied.

Cristelle sat forward in the taxi and pressed the phone to her ear. 'Did you just say in Paris?'

'That's right. I hope you don't mind my calling. I took the liberty of taking your number from Rose's bag.'

'Rose is also in Paris?' Cristelle asked, although here was a question that finally, she thought she knew the answer to.

'Yes,' said Henry.

'By any chance,' Cristelle said slowly, 'are you both staying at the Hotel Golden Tulip?'

Now it was Henry's turn to sound mystified. 'The very one,' he said. 'How...?'

'Oh, never mind,' said Cristelle. 'A lucky guess.'

'Right,' Henry said, happy to drop it. 'Well, the thing is, Cristelle, we wondered if you'd like to come to dinner with us.'

Cristelle didn't know what to say.

'It's just,' Henry paused, then cleared his throat and said quickly, 'Hannah would have celebrated another birthday three days ago. We'd like to celebrate on her behalf with, well, our family.'

Cristelle fought back imminent tears.

'Will Omega be there?' Cristelle asked.

'We thought we'd leave that decision up to you,' Henry answered.

'Where is he staying?' said Cristelle.

'In Montmartre,' Henry said. She could hear him shuffling some papers nearby. 'I, em, happen to have his number here if that might interest you.'

Despite herself, Cristelle laughed. 'It might,' she admitted. 'Did Rose put you up to this?'

'No,' said Henry truthfully. 'I thought it might be a nice surprise for her. She's in the shower. I know it's a lot to ask. And if you don't...then I'd – we'd – totally understand...'

'I have a pen here, Henry,' Cristelle cut in. 'And I'm ready to use it.'

L'Homme Tranquille

Rose and Henry sat peaceably in a small cosy restaurant on Rue des Martyrs.

'Isn't this pleasant?' Rose asked dreamily.

'Yes, dear,' Henry replied, surreptitiously glancing at his watch.

I Wish...

There was a call from reception to say Cristelle had arrived. Omega took the steps two at a time. When he got to the lobby, there was nobody there. He looked around him, trying not to panic. The guy behind reception motioned to the window.

She was waiting for him just outside, the pashmina they'd bought on their honeymoon wrapped snugly around her shoulders.

When he rounded the corner, she shrugged at him, and smiled.

Omega burst into tears.

Cristelle put her arm around him.

He howled.

'I wish I could cry,' she told him, laughing softly. 'I know I need to.'

'I wish I could be the man you deserve,' he said, his voice breaking. He dried his eyes roughly with his shirt-sleeves. 'All I know is how horribly, horribly sorry I am for the hurt I've caused you.'

'You *so* don't deserve me,' Cristelle agreed.

'The last thing Hannah ever said to me,' blubbed Omega, 'was to look after you. And I've totally messed up.' Tears were streaming down his face now and he was gulping like he couldn't get enough air.

An old man wearing a dark linen suit and a trilby hat was coming towards them, his hands clasped behind his back. Cristelle was surprised to see a daisy dangling from his mouth. He looked from one to the other in silent appraisal, then passed on.

She looked back at Omega; his body was still shaking uncontrollably.

'Look at us,' she said sadly. 'Two lost souls.'

'Swimming in a fish-bowl,' Omega managed to say, his mouth turned up into a painful smile.

'Where do we go from here?' asked Cristelle, cocking her head to one side and narrowing her eyes.

'This isn't where we intended to be,' Omega responded at once.

'We've got to make a decision,' said Cristelle, the first real smile breaking over her face like sunshine.

'Leave tonight or live and die this way,' Omega answered without hesitating.

They played the song-game until they got to the restaurant. It wasn't a real conversation, but it was a way into one.

Last Supper in Paris

'Shall we order, dear?' asked Rose.

'Umm,' said Henry, playing for time. 'Just not quite sure whether it will be the sea bass and steamed garden vegetables or the, em...' He glanced yet again towards the window.

'What on earth are you looking at, Henry?' said Rose, feeling a bit exasperated. She swivelled round in her chair just in time to see Omega and Cristelle crossing the street.

'Oh, Henry!' she said, her face lighting up.

A couple of days later, Omega described the evening over the phone to Dawn, how they ate and talked into the small hours, telling all their favourite stories of Hannah and Jack, and of her too, of course, and how at one point, fuelled by a few glasses of red wine, which he normally never touched, Henry had become suddenly expansive and amazed them all with a series of highly amusing anecdotes about his colleagues and his courting days with Rose.

'You mean the ice age?' joked Dawn.

'Well, before our time anyway,' laughed Omega.

They were silent for a while. Then Dawn said, 'Jack wants to know when you're coming back.'

'Put it like this,' Omega replied. 'I'm phoning from the airport.'

Homecoming

The automatic mirrored doors parted. Henry appeared first, dragging an old battered suitcase behind him. Then Rose, wearing a straw hat. Then Omega, looking like he hadn't slept for a week. Jack scanned the faces of the arriving passengers with an increasing sense of urgency. *Where was she?* He hopped up and down in an agony of anticipation. Suddenly he could be seen breaking away from Dawn and José-Maria, ducking under the silver railing and bolting through the doors, his runners emitting streaks of red light as they pounded the smooth polished floor. 'Hey, you!' shouted the guard. 'Stop!' But Jack was unstoppable. Cristelle was waiting for her last bag to come through. Next thing, she had a monkey on her back. The monkey put his paws over her shoulders and squeezed her neck so tightly she thought she was going to faint. She prised the paws apart and swung him round to get a better look. 'God, you've got heavy, Jack!' she laughed.

'They kept saying you were in Paris,' Jack told her in a very small voice. 'But I didn't believe them. I thought you'd gone to see Mommy and decided to stay with her and the angels.'

'Oh, Jack!' said Cristelle, laughing and crying at the same time. 'We'll all go see Hannah when the time comes. I promise. Just not today.'

Acknowledgments

I was the girl wearing the yellow polka-dot number, until a few people I'd like to thank helped persuade me to come out of the water: my agent of agents, Ger Nichol – without you, I wouldn't have written these acknowledgments. Deirdre Nolan of New Island, whose mellifluous voice kept me calm throughout the process. Niamh Ryan, my first reader, who gave me a spiral-bound notebook to bring to Paris with a picture of the Eiffel Tower on the front: I can't overstate how much I loved that notebook. Simonetta Giordano, cicerone of Paris, lion-hearted friend and confidante. My super-Gran F. Hurley, and Pop, who encouraged me in my poetry-writing habit. Big brother John, who sent me *The Catcher in the Rye* when I was a twelve-year-old geek in Irish college and helped raise my cool quotient. My sister Sarah and brother Patrick, for their constant support and encouragement. Giando, my dear heart.

This book is dedicated to my parents: after all that getting, it feels good to give.

The definition of make-up was reproduced from *Collins English Dictionary – Complete & Unabridged* with the kind permission of HarperCollins Publishers Ltd. © HarperCollins Publishers Ltd 1991, 1994, 1998, 2000, 2003, 2005, 2006. The description of the Natural History Musem was used with the kind permission of the National Museum of Ireland – Natural History.